T0328733

"HASHAYD!"

George struck into the woods, following the lilting music, brushing branches out of his way as he pressed forward. Rough pine needles scraped his fingers. It was darker in here, much darker than out on the path. He squinted, struggling to make sense of where he was going. *Damn.* He stumbled a few times. But there was a red glow ahead . . . the light of a fire nestled into the trees. The smoke grew thick. His eyes watered.

"Hashayd! Hashayd! Hashayd!"

All right. Now they were singing gibberish.

He froze.

Hold up. That's—

In a flash he ducked down, crouching behind a damp tree trunk. He *knew* that word. It wasn't gibberish. *Hashayd* was Hebrew for "the Demon." He was sure of it. Sarah had taught him a bunch of Hebrew words—back in August, when they had driven across the country together. They were all in that scroll of hers.

He was about to walk in on a bunch of Demon worshipers.

About the Author

Daniel Parker is the author of over twenty books for children and young adults. He lives in New York City with his wife, a dog, and a psychotic cat named Bootsie. He is a Leo. When he isn't writing, he is tirelessly traveling the world on a doomed mission to achieve rock-and-roll stardom. As of this date, his musical credits include the composition of bluegrass sound-track numbers for the film *The Grave* (starring a bloated Anthony Michael Hall) and a brief stint performing live rap music to baffled Filipino audiences in Hong Kong. Mr. Parker once worked in a cheese shop. He was fired.

COUNT DOWN

OCTOBER

by
Daniel Parker

Simon & Schuster

First Aladdin Paperbacks edition September 1999

Produced by 17th Street Productions,
a division of Daniel Weiss Associates, Inc.
33 West 17th Street, New York, NY 10011

Cover design by Mike Rivilis

Aladdin Paperbacks
An imprint of Simon & Schuster
Children's Publishing Division
1230 Avenue of the Americas
New York, NY 10020

ISBN: 978-1-4814-2595-7

To Jeff and Schuyler

OCTOBER

The Ancient Scroll
of the Scribes:

In the tenth lunar cycle,
At the dawn of the year 5760,
The countdown nears its end.
Both the Demon and the Chosen One are
weakened by a surge in the earth's energy.
A shift in the forces that empower
the Demon's secret and ancient weapon.
They fight bitterly, but neither is victorious.
The Seers are troubled by visions of the
approaching Final Battle, yet deceived.
Guided by the servants of the Demon
onward toward their fiery death.
The strongest among them are tested.
The blessed among them are
confused by the truth.
Even the False Prophet comes to
suspect his powers are failing,
And the Demon fills his heart with fear.

Depraved rats known to feed as one
soon bury lethal sins of killers.
Steal some tan cheese and sneak away.
Ten twenty-two ninety-nine.

The countdown has started . . .

The long sleep is over.

For three thousand years I have patiently watched and waited. The Prophecies foretold the day when the sun would reach out and touch the earth—when my slumber would end, when my ancient weapon would breathe, when my dormant glory would blaze once more upon the planet and its people.

That day has arrived.

But there can be no triumph without a battle. Every civilization tells the same story. Good requires evil; redemption requires sin. The legends are as varied as are the civilizations that spawned them—yet each contains that same nugget of truth.

So I am not alone. The Chosen One awaits me. The flare opened the inner eyes of the Visionaries, those who can join the Chosen One to prevent my reign. But in order for them to defeat me, they must first make sense of their visions.

For you see, every vision is a piece of a puzzle, a puzzle that will eventually form a picture . . . a picture that I will shatter into a billion pieces and reshape in the image of my choosing.

I am prepared. My servants knew of this day. They made the necessary preparations to confuse the Visionaries—all in anticipation of that glorious time when the countdown ends and my ancient weapon ushers in the New Era.

My servants unleashed the plague that reduced the earth's population to a scattered horde of frightened adolescents. None of these children know how or why their elders and youngers perished.

And that was only the beginning.

My servants have descended upon the chaos. They will subvert the Prophecies in order to convert the masses into unknowing slaves. They will hunt down the Visionaries, one by one, until all are dead. They will eliminate the descendants of the Scribes so that none of the Visionaries will learn of the scroll. The hidden codes shall remain hidden. Terrible calamities and natural disasters will wreak havoc upon the earth. Even the Chosen One will be helpless against me.

I *will* triumph.

PART 1:

October 1, 1999

CHAPTER ONE

**Babylon,
Washington
Morning**

The day was cold and drizzly—pretty damn typical for the Pacific Northwest—and Ariel Collins wasn't the least bit surprised. Nope. She had counted on lousy weather. Anyway, it could have been worse. *Much* worse. The last time she'd run away and come back home, she was practically buried alive in a swarm of grasshoppers. Then, of course, there was that time in July when blood fell from the sky.

So in a way, the rain was a relief. At the very least it gave the town a somewhat normal vibe. And that was quite a feat. It was a freaking miracle, in fact.

Ariel brushed a damp strand of brownish blond hair out of her eyes and sighed. It was strange that things looked so much the same: drab and colorless, like a black-and-white movie. The evergreens were wilting. On days like this, all the suburban houses looked as if they had been spewed out of the same cheap factory. They looked like toys.

The old 'hood, she thought bitterly. *Home, sweet home.*

Anger boiled inside her . . . at her town, at the

5

world, at her *life*. Maybe that was why she was so relaxed. Anger had always made her cool and calm. And she should have been scared, considering there was a very good chance she would be killed in the next five minutes.

Okay . . . maybe she didn't feel quite *so* calm. But there was something so familiar about this—as if every day were spent plodding down a deserted street with Leslie Tisch at her side, waiting to be attacked and murdered. It was kind of symbolic. The past five months had all been part of the same long march toward doom, hadn't they? There was no denying it. At this moment (with the exception of Leslie), everyone who had ever known Ariel wanted her dead.

Well, it wouldn't be long now. She could already see the sign, looming over the sidewalk on the next block. Washington Institute of Technology, Babylon Campus. She snorted. Too bad that sign didn't shed any light on what really went on there. It should have read: Trevor Collins's Dungeon of Horrors.

"How're you doing?" Leslie murmured. "You okay?"

Ariel stole a quick glance at her best friend. *You're asking me?* she wondered. In spite of everything, *Leslie* was the one who looked like she needed a sedative. The girl's skin was deathly white. Her long, dark curls shrouded her head. And she couldn't keep still. Her tattered umbrella trembled as she tried to hold it over both of them.

"Oh, you know, I'm doing pretty well," Ariel said after a minute. She made sure her tone was bright and cheerful. "I mean, the last time I saw all my old

6

friends, I got stabbed in the heart. Can't get much worse, right?"

Leslie didn't answer.

"Um . . . do you want me to hold that umbrella?" Ariel offered.

"No thanks. It's cool."

"Don't worry, Leslie," Ariel said. "I'm ready to roll the dice. Spin the wheel. Play the cards. Aces high, *baby* . . . to use your favorite word."

Leslie gave her a wan smile. Ariel swallowed. In fact, Leslie hadn't used the word *baby* in a very long time. But even in the face of all the horror, Ariel fought to keep a sense of humor. She *clung* to it. It was her security blanket, the one thing nobody could take from her. A sense of humor was what made people human, right? Maybe that was why the words *human* and *humor* were so similar. Being human meant having the ability to laugh, to see something funny in a situation—even if the circumstances were worse than anything imaginable.

I don't even know if I am human, though.

Her eyes wandered to the necklace around Leslie's neck.

It still seemed bizarre to think that her entire existence depended on that one lousy piece of metal—that ugly, silver ticktacktoe board. Not even—her entire existence depended on Leslie's *theory* of what the necklace could do. If Leslie was right, it meant that the necklace was responsible for all the terrible things that had happened to Ariel. The necklace had caused people who believed in the Chosen One to catch the melting plague whenever they got within ten feet of her. The necklace had kept her alive even with a knife in her heart, even in the middle of a deadly car crash. It possessed some kind of awful, magic power. The thought of it was crazy, beyond comprehension.

But it meant that Ariel was now in grave danger. Because she'd agreed to let Leslie hang on to the necklace for a while, just to prove her theory. And if Leslie was right, then Ariel was defenseless without the necklace. This time if somebody tried to kill her, Ariel would die.

Of course, maybe Leslie was wrong. Maybe Ariel was a demon. *The* Demon. That's certainly what everyone in Babylon thought.

Whoa.

Ariel stiffened, sniffing the air. Leslie did the same. They stood right outside the big stone campus wall, and there was a stench. . . . Ariel could barely breathe through the smell. To say that it reeked would be a *nice* way of putting it. It smelled as if every sewer in a ten-mile radius had simultaneously overflowed.

Hold on. . . .

Ariel knew that stink. Some guy they'd met on the road a couple of days ago had shoved a bunch of turnip bulbs in their faces, claiming it would cure the plague. She and Leslie had kept on walking, of course. The bulbs were really foul. But maybe he had been telling the truth. Maybe turnips *did* prevent everyone over twenty-one from turning into piles of black gook. Why else would people subject themselves to the odor?

"Is that . . . ?" Leslie didn't finish. She clamped her hand over her nose and shook her head. *"Jeez.* I didn't remember it being so nasty."

"Me neither," Ariel muttered, grimacing. She tried her best to breathe through her mouth. But the fetid smell was so overwhelming that she could actually *taste* it.

Leslie stepped forward and peered around the rough-hewn wall through the gate. "Hey, take a look at this."

Ariel tried to follow. But her feet seemed to be stuck to the wet cement sidewalk. She *wanted* to take a look at the campus—but she couldn't budge.

Visionaries lurked on the other side of that wall. Visionaries who wanted to kill her.

Some primitive instinct for self-preservation took control of her body. And it wasn't even motivated by a fear of losing her life. No, it was motivated by a fear of losing her *sanity.* Because if Leslie was wrong, if just *one* more crazed kid vaporized in front of her . . .

"Come on," Leslie urged. "Check it out."

"What . . . ah, what's going on?"

"There are a lot of people," Leslie murmured absently. "There must be hundreds of them. . . ."

Hundreds? Ariel held her breath and listened carefully. All she heard was the patter of raindrops on her head and on the sidewalk.

Why was it so quiet?

"I don't get it," Leslie whispered.

Okay, *now* Ariel was scared. Yup, she'd been lying to herself earlier. Her heart thumped. But she

9

clenched her fists at her sides and inched toward the edge of the gate, poking her head around the wall to see down the tree-lined drive.

My God.

She drew in her breath. The campus was unrecognizable. The barbed wire fence had been torn down. The main building was falling apart. Windows were broken, doors had been torn off their hinges, the paint was chipping . . . and the lawn was *mobbed,* crammed with kids who were crowded around a huge, smoky fire. If they were being cured of the plague, they sure didn't look it. They looked as if they were at a funeral.

Nobody was smiling. Nobody was even talking.

She shuddered. Something about the utter silence . . . it sent a chill down her spine. What was wrong? A few of the kids were staring up at a room on the second floor. The windows were dark—but if she strained her ears, she could almost hear a quavering wail, the sound of somebody crying. . . .

"What do you think?" Leslie asked, glancing back at her.

"I don't know," Ariel mumbled.

"You think your brother's still here?"

Ariel shook her head. "No way. Trevor would never let the place go down the tubes like this. He's a total neat freak. This was his *home,* remember? His pride and joy. His special little prison camp." The words oozed from her lips with contempt. Her apprehension faded. "I bet the Chosen One found out what he was doing to all the kids who believed in her. I bet

10

he got what he deserved." She laughed harshly. "After all, he's the Demon's brother—"

"You're *not* the Demon," Leslie snapped. "I'm sick of hearing it. Why do you keep—"

"Whatever," Ariel interrupted. "Even if I'm not, everybody in there thinks I am. Including Trevor. That's what matters."

"But that's why we're here!" Leslie cried. She grabbed the silver pendant with her free hand and held it up to Ariel's face. "We have to show all those people that the Demon put a spell on you and that this *thing* is what—"

"Shhh!" Ariel hissed. She withdrew her head and leaned against the cold, wet stone. Her pulse was racing. Now somebody had probably spotted her.

"We're not hiding anymore," Leslie stated. She planted herself in front of Ariel. Her dark eyes bored into Ariel's own. "You're going to have to deal with this. And I want to know the truth as much as *you* do. So suck it up and go in there."

Suck it up?

Ariel suddenly felt as if she were staring into a mask, as if a stranger had taken Leslie's place. Didn't she realize the danger—for *both* of them? Couldn't she show a little compassion?

"What?" Leslie demanded. "Why are you looking at me like that?"

"I—I think you should take the necklace off," Ariel found herself stammering. "I don't think it's a good idea for *anyone* to keep wearing it. I mean, what if the Chosen One freaks start melting whenever *you* get near them? Then they'll think *you're* the Demon."

11

"We've been over this, Ariel," Leslie said in a tired voice. "You can't have the necklace."

Ariel tried to take a step back, but she was already pressed against the wall. "I . . . I don't want it," she whispered. "I swear. I just want you to throw it out."

"You still want the necklace, Ariel. Face it. You're like an addict—that's just what Jezebel wanted." Leslie took a deep breath. "But I'll tell you what we'll do. We'll scope the place out before we talk to anyone. We'll make sure neither one of us gets close to any Visionaries—at least not until we figure out what's going on here."

Ariel didn't answer. She couldn't. She knew what Leslie was doing. She was trying to save Ariel—the way she had twice before. But this was different. This time Leslie herself was in terrible danger. If she was right about the power of the necklace, then Leslie would be the one who caused the COFs to vaporize—and they'd try to kill her.

But Leslie wanted to clear Ariel's name. She wanted to prove to the Visionaries that they had the wrong "Demon." She wouldn't be talked out of it.

And now as Ariel looked at her best friend, she had only one feeling.

Fear.

CHAPTER
TWO

Oakley,
Idaho
Afternoon

I know what my purpose in life is. It's to survive long enough to give birth to my baby. That's it. That's all I have to do. . . .

Branches lashed Julia Morrison's round stomach as she stumbled through the underbrush. She was sweating. The moisture beaded on her dark, weather-beaten skin—drenching her matted dreadlocks, stinging her eyes. There was no trail, no clearing. But it didn't matter. She'd made it to the bottom of the mountain. The temperature had climbed. The ground beneath her swollen ankles had leveled off. The trees were taller down here, towering high above her, blocking out the sun. It couldn't be long until she found a river, a road, *something*. She broke into a run. . . .

Uh-oh.

Her right foot plunged into the earth. But it didn't stop. Something swallowed it. A slimy coldness crept up her shins. She glanced down, but her belly protruded so far that she couldn't see her lower half. All she saw was watery, brown muck. And she was sinking in it. *Fast*. What was going on? Was it quicksand? Why couldn't she get free?

13

"Help me!" she shrieked.

Her cry rang through the empty forest. Screaming wouldn't do any good. She hadn't seen another living soul in . . . what? Two weeks? A month? Not since Luke had vaporized, leaving her lost and alone on that snowy mountaintop. For all she knew, she was the last person left alive on earth.

The mud inched toward her knees.

"Help!"

Her breath started coming fast. All right. She couldn't get hysterical. She was going to focus all of her energy on her leg. Yes.

She gripped her right thigh tightly, then took a deep breath.

You can do this. I know you can. You did it once before, when you were buried in that avalanche. Three . . . two . . . one . . .

"Agh!"

With a violent kick her foot popped free: *slurp*—but the motion sent her tumbling onto her backside. She winced as she plopped down into the mud. Now her tattered, filthy robe was soaked. *Soaked . . .*

When would it *end?* She couldn't even get up. She was too exhausted to move. When would she eat a decent meal, scrub the dirt that was caked between every toe and finger, put on some clean clothes? She'd lived on nothing but snow and berries for days. She didn't even want to *think* about what she'd been tempted to eat. And she could only imagine what the starvation and sleeplessness had done to the health of her baby.

All right. Enough. *There I go again, feeling sorry for myself.*

Her baby's father wouldn't wallow in this pitiful state. No, if George were alive, he would already be up, fighting his way out of the woods. So what if she was hungry? Hadn't George taught her anything? Hadn't he taught her to be tough? Besides, time was running out. Her visions grew sharper by the day. The sand was slipping through the hourglass. She still wasn't sure where she needed to be. Her baby's life depended—

Wait. What was that?

She froze, straining her ears. Had she heard a rustling sound?

". . . coming from over here," a faint voice called.

Julia's head jerked up. *People!* She opened her mouth to scream again—but all that came out was a hoarse gasp.

". . . gotta be her." It was a girl. "I saw it like this. . . ."

The rustling grew closer. Julia squirmed out of the ooze and lurched to her feet. "Over here!" she croaked. "Here . . ."

"There she is!" a boy cried. "I see her!"

There was movement in the bushes, maybe twenty feet to Julia's right. *Yes!* She started jumping frantically up and down, flailing her arms, flinging mud all over the place. "Here I am!"

A figure appeared out of the shadowy tangle of leaves: a boy with long blond hair, in a flannel shirt. He smiled and waved.

"We're coming, Julia!"

Julia? Her smile vanished. Her arms fell to her sides. She'd never seen that kid before in her life. She was sure of it. Was this part of some weird dream—a vision, maybe? No . . . it had to be real. She was sopping wet, cold, and in pain. She was very much awake. She could hear her heart pounding away under her ribs. The kid was followed by a girl . . . then another girl. All three were blond, stocky, ruddy cheeked. They must have been siblings. They looked like the Swiss Family Robinson or something. But who *were* they?

"I knew we were gonna find you!" the boy called excitedly.

Julia bit her lip. *Find me?* But nobody even knew she was alive—

Harold.

The brief flash of relief turned to horror. These kids had to be with Harold. He must be searching for her. He couldn't afford to let her get away. Of course not. She knew the truth: He wasn't the Chosen One; he was a fraud. In fact, it was sheer luck that he hadn't found her sooner. After all, she was being *drawn* somewhere . . . just like the other Visionaries, the ones whom Harold had fooled. So Harold only needed follow their lead to be reunited with Julia Morrison, "the heretic." He only needed to use his followers' visions *against* them—in the same sickening and perverse way he always had.

It was clever. Yes. Very, very clever.

Run! she commanded herself.

But it was too late. She was surrounded. There was no hope of escape. Blackness crept over the edges of her vision. A dizzying rush filled her ears. The three smiling blond faces swam before her eyes, multiplying

16

like talking heads on an ever-diminishing split screen: first six, then twelve, then dozens and dozens. . . .

Never before have I felt so peaceful.

I'm in the dark place. I'm standing beside the fire. The Chosen One stands with me. Her face is hidden.

"I must have died," I say. "Is that what happened?"

The Chosen One shakes her head. "No, Julia. That is not your destiny."

The fear returns; the contentment fades. The countdown is not over. I can tell by the sound of the Chosen One's voice. . . .

"I don't understand," I whisper. "What destiny?"

"You must destroy the Demon," she says.

And the Demon's face appears in the fire: horrible and monstrous, with a serpent's eyes and dripping flesh. My eyes turn from it. But in the black emptiness above the fire I see a strange symbol . . . a criss-cross pattern of slanted silver bars.

"You must drive your sword into her belly," says the Chosen One.

And then I remember: the desert, the hot sun, the battle I have seen a thousand times.

"How?" I ask.

"You'll know soon," the Chosen One answers. "Very, very soon."

Julia's eyes opened slowly. She yawned. At first she saw nothing but fuzzy shapes against a dazzling white backdrop.

17

And then, to her utter amazement, she realized something.

She was *comfortable.*

Except for the hunger gnawing at her stomach, she actually felt pretty decent. She was lying on her back, stretched out on something wonderfully soft and warm . . . a bed. A real, honest-to-goodness bed—with clean sheets and a fluffy down comforter. How long had it been since she'd slept in one of these? She sighed. Not in over seven months, not since she and George had found that little cabin . . .

Gradually the blurriness faded.

The bed was in a large and beautifully appointed room. There was a floor-to-ceiling mirror, a huge stereo system. The walls were covered with portraits. The ceiling must have been fifteen feet high. It looked like a set from a movie about the rich and famous. Maybe *now* she was dead. This could be heaven, right? It was definitely close enough. She nearly laughed out loud—until she saw something move out of the corner of her eye.

What the—

Those three blond kids were hovering over her.

"How do you feel, Julia?" the boy asked.

No! She tried to squirm away from them. But she ended up getting tangled in the sheets. She couldn't roll over; she didn't want to hurt the baby. . . .

"Relax," one of the girls murmured. "You're safe now—"

"You're with Harold!" Julia spat. In desperation she gathered the comforter around her body—as if *that* could possibly offer any protection.

The three of them exchanged puzzled glances.

"Um . . . who's Harold?" the boy asked.

"The one who sent you here," she growled.

A flicker of recognition passed over his face. "Wait, I think I get it. Harold's the False Prophet, right? You're running away from the False Prophet."

Julia didn't answer. She swallowed, studying each face—one at a time. Was it possible that these kids *weren't* with Harold? They weren't part of the flock. . . . But it must be a trick. A *clever* trick: the kind Harold would pull. Obviously her first instinct would be to relax, to let her guard down. That was what they wanted. It seemed a little *too* convenient that the boy had made an instant connection between Harold and the "False Prophet." And there was still the question of how they knew her name. . . .

"Listen to this," the boy said. "I want you to hear something."

He nodded to one of the girls.

She wordlessly padded across the room and pressed a button on the stereo.

". . . Chosen One is coming!" an excited voice cried from the speakers. "He heals all those in his path! Wait for him on the western slope of Mount Rainier! There you will receive his blessing!"

"I . . . I don't get it," Julia stammered, frowning. "What *is* that?"

The girl flicked off the power. "That's the False Prophet. He's spreading lies, Julia."

Stop saying my name!

"You're wondering how we know about you," the boy whispered. "Aren't you?"

19

"Of course I am," Julia practically whimpered. She felt like a caged animal.

"We see things. All of us. Me and my two sisters. When the plague killed our parents, we started having blackouts, visions." The boy smiled and sat on the edge of the bed. "We—"

Julia bristled.

"It's okay," he soothed. "See, we started seeing *you*. We all heard your name. We knew you'd come to us out of the woods. Every day, for months and months, we took walks and—"

"You're lying," Julia interrupted. "That's impossible."

The boy glanced back at his sisters. "But you have to believe us," he murmured. "We've been waiting for this day for a long, long time."

Every muscle in Julia's body tensed, poised for escape. "I don't hear any names in *my* visions," she snapped.

One of the girls leaned forward. She couldn't have been much older than sixteen. "Julia, do you know what this means for us?" she asked. Her voice was soft. "It's like . . . it's like, I don't know—meeting a legend or something." She blushed suddenly. "Oh, God—forget I said that." She turned away. "But it's like, we *know* you're one of the Blessed Visionaries. There are only two. And you're one of them."

Julia's eyes narrowed. "What do you mean?"

"*You* could see through the False Prophet's lies."

Me? No. An image of George flashed through her mind, as clearly as if she were looking at a photograph. She could see every detail of his face: those beautiful green eyes, that sweet smile, that

20

messy mop of blond hair. . . . *He* was the Blessed Visionary. The only one. Her heart squeezed. *He* was the one who had seen through Harold, long before she ever had. And it had cost them their relationship. A lump grew in her throat. Harold had blinded her—

"Listen to me, Julia," the girl went on. "We know all about you. We know about your daughter. She's the child of the Blessed Visionaries. The Chosen One will anoint her as her heir. She will lead those who defeat the Demon into a glorious New Era—"

"Shut *up!*" Julia howled. She couldn't listen anymore; she couldn't trust these kids. How did they know so much about her? How did they know she would bear a daughter? Julia herself wasn't sure. . . . But was she? She'd always had a feeling her baby would be a girl, although she'd never articulated it to anyone. Not even George. No, George had died without knowing that Julia was even pregnant.

"I'm sorry," the boy murmured. He stood quickly and ushered the two sisters to the door. "I know you're tired. You've been through a lot. We can talk later. Okay?"

Julia couldn't reply.

Tears began to stream down her cheeks. The memories of George were too much to handle. Her mouth opened in a silent wail. She shut her eyes. She only wanted to block everything out, to slip into unconsciousness, to *sleep.* . . .

The hourglass stands before me. It is taller now— taller than it has ever been. I can't even see the top of

21

it. I can only see the funnel. The last grains of sand are tumbling down. . . .

"Remember!" *the Chosen One shouts.* "Remember what you have seen and learned! The sword is a symbol! A symbol for the key!"

"What key?" *I cry. I turn in the darkness, but I am blind. The Chosen One's voice echoes at me from all directions. I can't find her—*

"Help!" Julia shrieked.

It took her a moment to realize she was sitting up in bed. Her face was moist. Her lungs were heaving. She blinked a few times, glancing around the luxurious room.

"Hello?" she called. Her voice trembled. "Hello?"

There was no answer.

What was going on? How much time had passed? She flung the comforter aside and swung her legs over the side of the mattress—

No. No. It can't be. . . .

Three identical piles of black sludge lay by the door. And on top of each were a pair of jeans, a pair of shoes, and a flannel shirt.

Julia was alone.

**Washington Institute of Technology,
Babylon, Washington
Late Afternoon**

"Are you sure you want to go in there?" Ariel whispered. "Maybe this isn't—"

"Don't be a wimp," Leslie mumbled. She inched a little farther down the dark, gritty hallway—toward the sound of muffled sobbing behind the closed classroom door.

"I'm not being a *wimp,*" Ariel replied. "I just think that if somebody locks themselves away in this place and cries for an entire day, they might want to be left alone."

Leslie pursed her lips but didn't reply.

Ariel sighed. Why had she let Leslie talk her into sneaking into WIT, anyway? There had to be another option. This deserted, broken-down lab was like a ghost town. And it wasn't the sound of the incessant crying that bothered her so much—or even the filth and disrepair. No, it was the memories. Trevor had imprisoned her in this place. He'd practically let her starve to death—he would have, if Leslie hadn't saved her. She couldn't stop thinking about it. She felt *sick.* A voice inside her head kept screaming for her to bolt back down the stairs and into the rain.

23

Maybe she *should* just leave.

Yeah. If Leslie wanted to harass some poor stranger, fine. She didn't need Ariel. Besides, they hadn't come any closer to figuring out why everybody was so bummed out around here. It made no sense—especially if the stuff in that stinking vat on the lawn really *did* cure the plague. Shouldn't those kids be throwing a party or something?

Leslie glanced back at Ariel. "Think I should knock?" she whispered.

"Whatever," Ariel muttered. "I'm gone."

"No, you're not."

Ariel blinked in surprise. She wasn't used to Leslie disagreeing with her or ordering her around.

"Don't you get it?" Leslie went on. "Something must have happened to the Chosen One. *That's* why things are so weird around here. And if we can talk to—"

The door flew open.

"Who are you?" a hoarse voice croaked. "What are you doing here?"

"We're—we're—," Leslie stammered.

A girl poked her head through the doorway. She looked about Ariel's age—long brown hair, pale skin, glasses. It was obvious from her puffy red eyes and damp cheeks that *she* was the one who had been crying all afternoon. The girl glared at Leslie. Ariel bowed her head and waited. This was the first person—besides Leslie—that she'd gotten within ten feet of since coming back to Babylon. Would this girl melt like all the others used to? Would she be the one to prove once and for all that Ariel was the Demon, necklace or no necklace?

"Oh, my God! Ariel! It's you!"

Without any warning, the girl dashed across the hall and swept Ariel up in an embrace.

What the hell? Ariel froze, too shocked to move. Her eyes widened. The girl was practically crushing her.

"I'm so sorry," the girl wept. She buried her face in Ariel's neck.

"Sorry for *what?*" Ariel murmured, cringing slightly. "Who are you?"

The girl stepped back. Her eyebrows were knit. "You don't know?"

"Uh . . ." Ariel shook her head.

"I'm Sarah Levy." She hesitated, letting her hands fall away from Ariel. "I'm the Chosen One."

Ariel exchanged a baffled glance with Leslie. Okay. Now the day had gone from lousy to just plain weird. The Chosen One? *Please.* How dumb did Ariel look? This girl was . . . well, for want of a better word, she was a dork. And the Chosen One wouldn't hug Ariel as if she were a long-lost friend. No, the Chosen One would probably burst out of the sky in a flaming chariot and strike Ariel dead with a bolt of lightning. Or *something.* Ariel Collins was supposed to be the Chosen One's mortal enemy, for God's sake. At least according to everyone around here.

"How do you know my name?" Ariel finally asked.

The girl sniffed. "I saw you once before. And you . . . you look just like your brother." She choked on the last word. Her face grew pained.

25

"You know Trevor?" Ariel asked, flabbergasted.

"Oh, my God. You don't—" The girl's voice broke. She started shaking. Tears streamed down her cheeks. "Come here," she whispered. She took Ariel's arm and led her gently toward the door. "You don't know yet, do you?"

Know what? Ariel wondered. But she didn't even bother to resist. She couldn't; she was too confused. She shuffled past Leslie into the classroom.

"There he is," Sarah whispered.

Trevor!

Ariel's insides turned to liquid. She clamped a hand over her mouth. *Oh, my—*

Her brother lay in a corner of the classroom, staring up at the ceiling with eyes that had turned a glassy brown. They looked like marbles. His skin was the color of sand. An ugly brown stain covered the top half of his white button-down shirt. In the center of it was a perfectly round black hole. Her brother was dead.

"What happened?" Ariel gasped.

"The Demon shot him," Sarah sobbed. "She killed him."

Cold numbness seized Ariel. *That's it. I'm all alone. My whole family is gone now. I'm the only one left. . . .*

"Hey!" Leslie's voice drifted in from the hall. "Did you say the *Demon?*"

Sarah nodded and rubbed her eyes. "Jezebel," she croaked, sniffling. "She came in here and stole my scroll. It was written in the prophecies that she would steal the key to the Future Time, and she did it right

26

in front of me. I was so stupid. She shot Trevor in the heart and—"

"Whoa, slow down," Leslie interrupted. She bounded into the room and grabbed Sarah's shoulder. "You say that *Jezebel* is the Demon? How do you know?"

Time seemed to freeze. Ariel couldn't make sense of what was being said. Jezebel had killed Trevor? Jezebel was . . .

Sarah stared at Ariel. Her face softened. "It would take too long to explain. But I know for sure that Ariel *isn't* the Demon. The prophecies said that the Demon would use magic to draw attention away from herself—"

"See!" Leslie shouted. She whirled and pulled Ariel against her, squeezing her in a tight hug. "I told you! She used the necklace to make everyone think *you* were the Demon—to keep the attention off her! Don't you know what this means? It's *over!*"

Ariel hung like a marionette in Leslie's arms, limp and motionless. How could Leslie be so happy? Was she *blind?*

"What's the matter?" Leslie cried. She held Ariel at arm's length. "Aren't you psyched?"

"Psyched?" Ariel gaped at her. "My brother's *dead,* Leslie."

"Yeah, and good riddance," Leslie muttered. Her tone was casual, almost jokey. She paused, then peered at Ariel as if she were insane. "Come on. He tried to *kill* you. He spread all those lies about you." She hesitated, searching Ariel's face. "You wanted him dead! You said so yourself this morning! He got what he deserved."

Ariel's eyes flashed back to her brother's corpse.

Bile rose in her throat. *My God.* She *had* said those things, hadn't she? Yes. And at the time she might have even meant them. . . . But she never really believed he would die. She never wanted this: to see him murdered and left to rot in this dirty classroom, like some animal carcass.

"Trev-Trevor was so . . . so sorry, Ariel," Sarah stammered. "It drove him crazy how you hated him. He blamed himself. When he learned the truth about Jezebel, he swore he would patch things up. He wouldn't stop talking about you." Her voice fell to a whisper. "He . . . he told me that he didn't think you killed your mom on purpose. He was so mixed up. He hated how you were so popular and always got what you wanted. . . ."

The words faded into nothingness. Ariel couldn't stand to listen to Sarah anymore. The pain was too great. She stared at the floor, clenching her teeth, fighting with every ounce of her strength to stay in control. She would *not* cry.

Maybe Leslie was right. Hating her brother was a lot easier than loving him, wasn't it? And she *did* hate him. For eleven long years they had barely spoken. They had no relationship. None. He had spurned her, attacked her, abused her in the most heinous and inhuman ways imaginable. Even if he was sorry, she could never forgive him.

Could she?

I hate you, Trevor. I hate you—

All at once, she burst into tears.

She wasn't even conscious of how it started. One

moment she was fine; the next she was huddled against Sarah, bawling like an infant. But she wasn't crying for Trevor . . . at least, not as he was now. Not for the twenty-year-old monster. She was crying for the little boy who was her playmate, back when their mother was still alive—back when Ariel's best friend lived down the hall in her very own house.

"It's okay, Ariel," Sarah soothed. "It's okay."

Ariel shook her head. "It's not," she wept. "I never—"

"But it was *his* fault!" Leslie shouted. She started pacing around the room, shaking her head. "Why are you on some guilt trip? That guy tried to kill you. *And* me. Personally, I'm pretty stoked he's gone. At least the Demon did *one* good thing—"

"Shut up!" Ariel shrieked. She staggered away from Sarah and thrust a shaky finger at Leslie. "You didn't even *know* him! And neither did Jezebel!"

Leslie rolled her eyes. "Whatever. But speaking of Jezebel . . ." She strode over to the window and shoved it open. The necklace clattered awkwardly against the sill. "Hey, everyone!" she shouted to the mob on the lawn. "Up here!"

What is she doing? Ariel's nostrils were instantly suffused with the foul odor of the boiling turnip bulbs. *Yechh.* She flinched, clutching at her nose.

"Just for the record, Ariel Collins is *not* the Demon!" Leslie barked. She jumped back, grabbed Ariel, and dragged her roughly across the room. "Take a good look at her, people! A good, long look. She is *not* the Demon! The Chosen One said so herself!"

Hundreds of shocked faces swam before Ariel's eyes—blurry and charcoal gray in the rain. She hardly knew what was happening. Leslie's fingers dug into her arm. She couldn't deal with this. She had to get out of here: to think, to *grieve*. But she didn't want to be alone. No, even as her head spun, as anger and sadness tore her in a dozen directions, she couldn't help but search for one person in the crowd—one face, with droopy blue eyes and broad lips. . . .

Caleb.

She hadn't allowed herself to think of him until now. But she *needed* him. If Trevor wanted to patch things up, wouldn't her old boyfriend want to do the same? Yes. He would. . . .

Only he didn't seem to be out there.

"Hey," Ariel sputtered. She spun and twisted free of Leslie's grasp. "Hey, Sarah. Do you know a guy named Caleb Walker?"

Sarah nodded.

"You do!" A surge of hope flashed through her. "Do you know where he is?"

"No." Sarah bit her lip, as if she were frightened of what she was going to say next.

"What?" Ariel pressed. "What's wrong?"

"He's gone. I haven't seen him since Jezebel disappeared."

Old Pine Mall,
Babylon, Washington
Night

Caleb Walker knew that he was in big trouble.

For one thing, there was no electricity at the mall, and he had stupidly brought just one candle to light his way. It had already shrunk to a formless glob in his hand. Bits of hot wax kept splattering on the floor. He figured he had about five minutes left. If he didn't find Jezebel in that time, he wouldn't be able to see a thing. Not that he could see much now.

No, that wasn't quite true. In some ways, he could see more clearly than ever. He'd had a revelation today: a moment of clarity where everything fell into place. It was as if he'd taken some kind of mind-altering drug. He'd learned something about himself—something very important.

Until now, he had never felt *guilt* before. Real, stabbing, all-consuming guilt. The kind that made your whole body clench up and freeze.

But then, he had never really felt much of *anything*.

Even before the plague, even before the long months of booze-addled debauchery, he had

31

always sort of coasted through life. It was so much easier that way. Why stop and examine the pathetic state of your existence? Better to block out the bad stuff: to laugh, to crack another beer, to do another shot. . . . His mom always told him: "Ignore something, and it will go away." That was what he did with his feelings. Good old Mom. He'd carved himself an entire personality out of helpful clichés like that. And he'd always skipped asking the kinds of questions that other spineless lowlifes probably asked themselves—namely: *How many lives have I destroyed?* and *Do I have any kind of morals at all?*

"Jezebel!" he shouted. The word reverberated across vast halls, lingering in the still air for several seconds: ". . . *ebel . . . ebel . . . ebel . . .*"

No answer. *Crap.* Maybe this was a mistake. He didn't even know if she was here. There was a very good possibility that she had sprouted wings and flown back to hell—

Stop it. He shook his head. *Don't freak out.* He had always been either too brave or too stupid to panic. It was his only redeeming quality, in fact. But he couldn't prevent the candle from shaking. The flame danced wildly at the end of the wick, swaying from side to side. He paused for a moment and took a deep breath.

Jezebel had *not* turned into some kind of all-powerful, magical . . . *thing.*

He had to keep reminding himself of that. The Demon had possessed her body . . . but she was still a *person.* She might be able to read minds, but that was it. She couldn't change shape or leap tall buildings in a single bound. After all, she needed a gun to kill Trevor, right? The Chosen One had spelled it out for him: The Demon had assumed a *human* form. *Human.* That was the key word. Caleb was a human, too. A no-good, idiotic human, sure—but at least they were evenly matched.

Unless she wants to shoot me.

No. She wouldn't shoot him. She *wanted* him. She had told him that the only thing standing in their way was Sarah's weird scroll. The ancient prophecies had turned him against her. But now that she had stolen the scroll, there were no more obstacles. And he was going to convince her that he didn't care who or what she was. No, he was going to tell her that he wanted *her,* too—because he admired her power, because he was tired of geeks and weaklings. He liked to party. To fool around. To have fun. So did she.

And as soon as her guard was down, he was going to kill her.

Careful, he reminded himself. *Don't think about your plan. If she's around here, she'll look into your head and see your thoughts. You have to convince yourself of the lie as you convince her.*

There was no doubt he could do it. He was an expert at lying to himself. A bitter smile spread across his lips. He'd done it his whole life. Luckily all the BS and self-deception could finally serve a purpose. It would give meaning to his otherwise worthless eighteen years. It would be his *redemption.* Killing Jezebel was all he had left to live for. He would avenge Trevor's death. He would destroy the Chosen One's enemy. He would do it for all the kids who had managed to survive this long. For the *future.*

And most of all, he would do it for Ariel—for all the crap he and everybody else had put her through because they thought *she* was the Demon. Jezebel had fooled them all.

Not for much longer, though.

His fingers tightened around the candle. "Jezebel!" he shouted again. "Jez—"

The flame abruptly vanished.

Dammit. He must have yelled too hard and blown it out. Now he was blind. He bit his lip, blinking in the velvety blackness. Should he try to feel his way to the wall? Or should he just sit his butt down on the marble floor and wait until morning?

"Caleb?" Jezebel's faint voice drifted out of the abyss. "Is that you?"

His heart jumped. *She's here!* Relief and terror gripped him at once. He dropped the sticky remnants of the candle and cupped his hands around his mouth. "Hey, Jez!" he called. "I'm by that toy store near the food court—"

A door squeaked open. Orange light flickered at the end of the corridor. Moments later Jezebel swung unsteadily around the corner—gripping a flaming torch in one hand and a small, dark bottle in the other.

Caleb fought the urge to smile. *Perfect.* She was wasted. Her defenses were down.

"What're *you* doin' here?" she slurred.

"I came to find you. I figured you'd be here. You always end up at the mall."

She staggered up to him. The bottle swished loudly.

He gave her a quick once-over. She looked awful. Her dark hair was a tangled mess. The black dress she always wore was fraying at the seams. And the sickly sweet odor of peppermint schnapps hung around her like smog. She swayed unsteadily from side to side, sneering. Then she belched.

"Are you okay?" he murmured. "You don't . . ."

All at once she straightened. "Don't worry, Caleb."

What the—

Her voice had abruptly changed. It was crisp, sharp, sober. She laughed and brushed the hair out of her glittering dark eyes. "I'm not drunk," she said. "I just wanted to know what you were really thinking. *Your* defenses are down. Not mine."

Caleb's jaw dropped.

"Just a little trick," she said with a smirk. "Haven't you ever seen those old kung fu movies with Jackie Chan? You know . . . *Drunken Master* and *Drunken Master II*?" She raised her eyebrows. "No? Too bad. They're classics. Jackie Chan pretends to be drunk so he can fool his enemies into thinking that he's weak. Then he kicks their asses. You'd be surprised how effective it is."

"I—uh, I—," he stammered. He had no idea what to say. His knees turned to water. What had he been thinking? Hadn't he learned what a devious bitch she could be? He shouldn't have come here. He'd

35

been right earlier. It was a big mistake. . . .

Jezebel's nose wrinkled. "Yes, Caleb. What *were* you thinking by coming here?"

He swallowed. *Just stay cool,* he ordered himself. He had to tell the truth—at least, as much as he possibly could. It was the only way to survive. "I wanted to talk to you," he finally managed. "You know—about . . . stuff."

"Stuff," she repeated flatly. "Always the articulate one, aren't you? So what kind of *stuff* did you want to discuss?"

Caleb hesitated. *Not good.* He was wrong; the only way to survive was not to think at all. "I missed you," he found himself blurting out. "I missed hanging out and getting smashed."

"Really." Her eyes narrowed. "I was under the impression that you quit drinking."

"Oh, yeah?" He snatched the bottle from her hand, threw back his head, and began to guzzle. *Blecch.* The peppermint schnapps tasted like cough syrup. Worse, in fact. He nearly gagged as it went down . . . until the liquor hit his gut in a delicious explosion. Jezebel was right, of course. He'd tried to quit; he hadn't had a drink in over a month. But he *did* miss it. Riding the wave of that familiar buzz was like slipping into a pair of favorite shoes. The fit was still perfect. Within seconds he already felt more relaxed, more confident.

"You're welcome," Jezebel muttered sarcastically. "Always the charmer, huh?"

"Whatever." He wiped his mouth with his sleeve, then started slugging again.

36

"Did you know that Ariel was back in town?" Jezebel asked.

Good God. His throat clenched. He spat out the booze and doubled over, choking for air.

Jezebel giggled. "I guess not."

"I don't want to see her," he gasped, straightening.

"Oh, come on—"

"I *don't*," he interrupted. "I want to stay here with you."

For a few seconds Jezebel just smiled. "Really?" she finally asked. "Even though I shot your new best friend?" Her voice hardened. "Even though that witch Sarah fooled you into believing that I'm the Demon?"

Caleb sighed. "Trevor was *not* my new best friend," he said. "I just went to him 'cause I was scared. I was scared of the Chosen One." He shoved Ariel from his thoughts. He couldn't believe how *mellow* he felt all of a sudden. The high seemed to spread to his extremities in warm, tingly waves. "But I learned something." He grinned at her.

"What was that?" Jezebel asked, sounding bored.

"*You're* just as powerful as Sarah is."

She eyed him skeptically. "What makes you say that?"

"You got the scroll, didn't you?" He took another sip. "You won. You kept Trevor from cracking that code Sarah kept talking about. Listen . . . you wanna know something? I *do* think you're the Demon. But I don't give a crap. I want to be on your side."

"I'm not the Demon," she said quietly. But her voice had lost its edge.

Caleb shrugged. "Like I said, I don't care one way or the other."

She lowered her eyes. "Doesn't it bother you that I'm, you know . . . *bad?*"

"Bad?" Caleb laughed. "Come on. What about me? We're both bad, Jezebel. Because bad is *fun*. That's why we have such a good time together." His voice rose; he felt as if he were listening to somebody else—somebody playing the role of Caleb Walker in a fantasy. But at the same time he truly believed what he was saying. It wasn't a lie, necessarily. And the more he talked, the more he bought it. "We're outcasts. Those Chosen One freaks are boring. None of that stuff matters anymore, anyway. We found a cure for the plague. We're all gonna live." He slapped his bulging pockets. "I got enough bulbs here to last me until I'm seventy years old."

Jezebel looked up at him. "What about me?"

He blinked a few times. "What about you?"

"Don't I get any of those bulbs?"

Oops. "Yeah, yeah. I mean, of course." He flashed an awkward smile. "I just—uh, I didn't think you needed them. . . ."

She grabbed the bottle from him and took a sip. "You'd get lonely if you grew old without me," she mumbled. "I know *I'd* get lonely without you. . . ."

"Come here," he said thickly.

He pulled her into his arms and pressed his lips against hers.

38

She didn't resist.

And amazingly enough, kissing her felt pretty good. Because part of him still enjoyed it. So he figured he'd focus on that part. Yeah, he'd stay nice and plowed . . . and lock the rest of his feelings—the anger and hatred and disgust—deep in some other hidden place.

PART II:

October 2-22

**Mount Rainier National Park,
Washington
Night of October 3**

"Happy birthday to you," George sang softly to himself. "Happy birthday to you. You smell like a monkey . . . and you look like one, too."

He allowed himself a grim chuckle as he gazed up through the evergreens at the bright moon. He really did smell like a monkey, didn't he? Just for the hell of it, he sniffed the sleeve of his grubby leather jacket. Yeah. Pretty rank. Not that it was a big shock. He'd been *living* like a monkey for the past month: hanging around this mountain, climbing trees, surviving off the scraps he found in the garbage bin at the tourist center—

Smack!

He winced. *Damn.* That invisible hand was slapping him again. He rubbed the back of his neck. It was really sore back there. And right after the slap came the pull. . . . *There it is!* He grimaced, pressing his hands against his bony rib cage. It was like a giant suction cup, yanking his lungs and heart and guts back toward the Chosen One. He shut his eyes and clenched his jaw. His breath came in quick gasps. *Fight it, fight it, fight*

43

it, he chanted silently. It was the only thing to do to get through the pain. . . .

Hell of a way to turn seventeen, wasn't it? Maybe he should just—

The pull eased up a little.

Whew.

George shook his head. His breathing evened. He wiped the sweat from his brow. Luckily the really bad agony never lasted more than a couple of seconds. He always felt a *little* tug—but ignoring that was just a matter of willpower.

There was no way in hell he would give in to the pain and go back to Babylon. Not without Julia. He could take it. Harold would show up here sooner or later. And Julia would be with him. "The Chosen One is coming! Wait for him on the western slope of Mount Rainier! There you will receive his blessing!" Yeah, right. Harold was just scheming to get all the Visionaries in one place so the Demon could take care of them. Those radio messages were a trap, a setup to kill the Seers. . . .

Don't think about Julia, you dope.

He sighed and shoved his hands into his pockets. Maybe he should go for a walk. He could warm up a little, clear his head.

Or maybe he should just go to the Paradise Inn and crash in a nice, cozy bed.

Yeah . . . that sounded good. The only problem was that he might run into somebody. He'd bumped into a few kids there last week. They'd all heard Harold's bull on the radio, too. And they believed it. They were hanging around, waiting for Harold's "blessing." George hadn't told them they were making a mistake, either. He had just split. He didn't want to attract any attention to himself. For all he knew, those kids could have been *spies* for Harold. And Harold still thought that George was dead, vaporized into black gook back at his farm.

So did Julia.

Screw it, George said to himself. It was his birthday. He deserved a treat. So what if he ran into somebody? He didn't have to tell them anything. He tucked his head down into his coat and started hiking down the moonlit trail, back down toward the tourist center. The truth was that he didn't want to be by himself tonight. It was too goddamn depressing.

Funny. His birthdays *always* sucked. Even when the world was normal.

Like the last one. . . . He remembered it so clearly: He'd gotten his license, but his foster father wouldn't let him drive. The old man *had* to be a jerk. So George took matters into his own hands. He hot-wired a killer BMW: a Z3, a two-seater convertible. Unfortunately Eight Ball was with him, and the fat fool started playing with the headlights—flicking them on and off. And what do you know? A cop started chasing them. So they had to ditch the car and hide under a truck in some parking lot. They spent an hour facedown on the pavement, breathing gas fumes, trying to be quiet. What a party.

George snickered. He kicked at the dirt as he walked. In a weird way, it was a good thing those days were over. At least he didn't hang with two-bit morons like Eight Ball anymore. And nobody could lock him down in the pen. No, he had a whole new set of problems now: visions, a Demon, a missing girlfriend who didn't even know he was alive. . . .

Hmmm.

He sniffed the air.

There was a scent. . . . It smelled like burning leaves.

Yeah. He picked up his pace. Maybe somebody was having a cookout or something.

His belly growled. He strained his ears, listening for the sound of voices over the crickets and his own footsteps.

The scent grew stronger.

He broke into a jog. *Whoa.* For a second he thought he heard . . . was it *singing?* He listened as carefully as he could as he flew down the dank path. *There*—off in the woods to the right. It *was* singing: a sweet, high-pitched melody, drifting on the wind. And from what he could tell, the voices sounded female. A bunch of girls having a sing-along. He laughed out loud. Hell, it was like camp. Not that he really knew what camp was like. The closest he'd ever come was a juvenile correctional facility.

". . . *kissing all the universe,*" one of the voices sang.

George frowned. That was kind of a weird line.

Sort of psychedelic. He'd never heard this song before. He struck into the woods, following the lilting music, brushing branches out of his way as he pressed forward. Rough pine needles scraped his fingers. It was darker in here, much darker than out on the path. He squinted, struggling to make sense of where he was going. *Damn.* He stumbled a few times. But there was a red glow ahead . . . the light of a fire nestled into the trees. The smoke grew thick. His eyes watered.

"Hashayd! Hashayd! Hashayd!"

All right. Now they were singing gibberish.

He froze.

Hold up. That's—

In a flash he ducked down, crouching behind a damp tree trunk. He *knew* that word. It wasn't gibberish. *Hashayd* was Hebrew for "the Demon." He was sure of it. Sarah had taught him a bunch of Hebrew words—back in August, when they had driven across the country together. They were all in that scroll of hers.

He was about to walk in on a bunch of Demon worshipers, wasn't he?

The blood drained from his face.

What the hell had he been *thinking?*

He should have known something was up the second he smelled the fire. Didn't he remember what happened the last time he found some weird girls hanging out in the middle of nowhere? He'd barely escaped with his life. And *this* wasn't the middle of nowhere, either. It was a very specific place: right where the Demon was setting her trap.

"Baruch Hashayd!"

Dizzying nausea flooded his empty stomach. *So stupid. So freaking stupid.* As cautiously as he could, he peered around the side of the tree. He caught a glimpse of hooded black shadows, dancing wildly against the hazy firelight—and immediately withdrew his head. His heart thudded. If there was any doubt left in his mind that these girls worshiped the Demon, it had just vanished. The Chosen One always referred to Demon worshipers as "the girls in black robes." And there they were: right smack in front of him.

"Black moon, Lilith, mare of night!" a girl cried.

All right. Just chill. Don't panic. They didn't see you. He held his breath, staring at nothing, blinking rapidly. He had to get back to the path. Fast. Silently. *Now.*

"You cast your litter to the ground," the girl continued. "Speak the Name and take to flight; utter now the secret sound!"

He fell to his hands and knees and began to slither across the forest floor. The cold mud felt good against his hot skin. He shivered. Rocks and branches tore at his clothes—

"Angro-mainyeush!" another girl shouted.

Oh, man. George's eyes bulged. That voice. It was sickeningly familiar. Was that Amanda, that psycho chick from Ohio? No. Impossible. She had been *killed.* He'd seen it with his own eyes. Julia had lit her hair on fire—

"Atha zamyut yatha afrinami!" the same girl cried.

It *was* her, wasn't it? George remained motionless. He could never forget that sultry tone, that huskiness. She sounded like a call girl. Should he look? Every second he wasted here put his life at risk. Still, he just had to take one last peek behind him. He had to see. . . .

Steeling his nerves, he glanced over his shoulder.

"Baruch Hashayd!" the entire crowd chanted.

But all he saw was a blur of formless black shapes, dancing around the fire.

No, something else caught his eye. It was hanging from a tree, suspended right above the flames: a sculpture. . . . It looked like a huge ticktacktoe board—only it was slanted, like the pound button on a phone. He'd seen that before, too.

He licked his dry lips. The Demon had been wearing it around her neck, right below the knife sticking out of her chest. *Ariel.* That was what the kids in Babylon called her. Not Lilith, or *Hashayd* . . . or *Angro-Mainyeush.* Why did the Demon have so many names? Was it to confuse people?

"Let us prepare for the False Prophet!" a different girl cried. "Harold Wurf is on his way, guided by the hand of Lilith!"

Damn. He'd seen enough. Anytime Harold's name came up, he felt like puking. It was time to haul ass out of here. But this was the first time he'd actually heard concrete *proof* that Harold was a fraud. It didn't really mean a thing, though. George didn't need to hear it. He had known the truth for months. His face twisted in anger.

Somebody else should have been here. Like Julia . . .

"Let us praise Harold Wurf!" the first voice shouted. "Let us shower him with burnt offerings! We light a flame for the foolish genius! For Lilith's unwitting servant! For the Healer and his mission to redeem humanity!"

The girls hooted with laughter.

What were they talking about? Foolish genius? George scowled. That made no sense.

"Yes, to Harold Wurf," said the girl who sounded like Amanda. Her tone was dry. "Our greatest pawn. He deserves our gratitude. Such a poor, confused soul. So easily persuaded of his *powers.* . . ." Her voice was lost in another round of wicked giggling.

Holy crap. Was this for real? In spite of his terror, George almost felt like laughing, too. Harold was being played? Like all the rest of them? No way . . .

"He doesn't deserve gratitude," somebody else chimed in. "He deserves sympathy."

George nodded. So it was true: Harold was Lilith's chump. But how was that possible? All those phony miracles . . . Did Harold really believe that *he* had pulled them off? That meant Harold wasn't a liar—at least, not in his own mind. He had no idea that the Demon and these chicks were calling the shots for him. Ha! George almost felt sorry for the guy.

Almost.

He took one last look at the fire, shook his head, then scrambled back into the night.

Harold Wurf was a sucker! He wanted to scream it at the top of his lungs. *Thank you, ladies. That's the best news I've heard in months. I can't wait to tell him when he shows up.*

Amazing. In spite of his almost getting killed, his birthday hadn't turned out so bad after all.

**Medicine Mountain,
Wyoming
October 4**

Dr. Harold Wurf didn't expect to miss his flock. Not in the least. He was *relieved* when they had split off into tiny groups, heading in a thousand directions, spreading his gospel to every survivor left in America. He'd had enough of them for a while.

Certainly, though, he figured he might miss the adulation. And the glory. And the *high* of dazzling a throng of hundreds. He didn't mind the perks, either: particularly the lovely teenage girls who would sacrifice anything for a single intimate encounter with the Chosen One. Yes, yes. The list stretched all the way back to January—beginning with Larissa, then Caroline. . . . He couldn't remember all of the names; there were too many.

Yet the fact remained that most of his followers were imbeciles. *Especially* the females. At any rate, he would see them all again at the end of next month on Mount Rainier—along with thousands more . . . and there his entire flock would be transformed by the mysterious power of his divine hand. He would bestow the gift of immortality upon them. Together they would usher in the glorious New Age.

Until then, however, he thought he would be perfectly content to remain with Linda.

Just Linda.

He would finally have a chance to consummate their relationship. He would finally know the pleasure of touching that tall and curvaceous body, of running his fingers through those blond curls, of gazing deeply into those blue eyes. . . .

Or so he had assumed.

But for three weeks now, she had politely refused all of his advances. Not that he was forcing himself on her. Still, he made quite a few subtle suggestions. Why not share a sleeping bag, for warmth? Why not hold hands, so as not to get separated? The answer was always no. A *nice* no, a *smiling* no . . . but a no all the same. And the more she rejected him, the more desirable she became. His need to have her was literally like fire in his blood. He couldn't look at her anymore without getting flushed, hot, distracted. He didn't understand it. She *worshiped* him. She was his most fervent believer. So why didn't she want to take their relationship as far as it could possibly go? Why didn't she want to become *one* with him—the way all the others had?

Linda wasn't like the others, though. She wasn't even American. Some miracle had plucked her out of England right before the plague and dumped her in his lap. . . .

"Harold?"

He jerked slightly. She was staring at him. He glanced at her, then turned back to the empty highway.

Ugh.

A cloud of sour gloom infected his thoughts. He didn't feel like walking anymore. Why bother? Nothing lay ahead but more cracked pavement, another deserted town or decrepit farmhouse . . . loneliness and frustration. He was sick of trying to put on a happy face for her sake. This trip was such a waste. *I can't take the monotony. I'm losing my mind. I should just hitchhike on my own. I should go straight to Mount Rainier—*

"Is something the matter?" she murmured.

"The matter?" He laughed harshly. "I should ask *you* the same thing."

She shook her head. "I don't understand—"

"Do you find me attractive, Linda?" he demanded. He stopped and glared at her. "Well?"

Her jaw dropped. She looked stricken. "I . . . I, uh—I don't . . ."

"It's a simple question," he spat. His pulse picked up a beat. "Do you or don't you?"

"Of course . . . of course I do," she whispered. Her expression softened. "You're *beautiful*. You're the Savior, the Chosen One—"

"No, no, no," he growled. He stamped the ground impatiently. "I'm not talking about that. Look, just . . . just *forget* that I'm the Chosen One, okay? For a second just try to look at me as another person. A twenty-year-old man. Do you think I'm good-looking?"

She blinked a few times, then flashed a confused smile. "I can't think of you like that, Harold. It's impossible. You *are* the Chosen One."

"Then why do you keep calling me *Harold?*" he cried. His face reddened. "Nobody else in the flock ever calls me Harold, except the nonbelievers. You *must* think of me as a normal person, right? Otherwise you'd call me the Healer—the way the rest of them do."

"Is that it?" she whispered. She stepped forward and laid her delicate fingers on his arm. Her face was creased with worry. "Have I offended you in some way? I didn't mean—"

"Oh, just . . . never mind." He shook free of her hand and stalked down the highway. How could she be so perceptive one minute and so *clueless* the next? What would it take? Would he have to tear off his clothes and confess his infatuation for her in the nude? What was *she* missing that the others hadn't?

"Harold, wait!" she called, running after him. "I'm sorry!"

But he didn't slow down. He quickened his pace and kept a few steps ahead of her. And he made up his mind right then and there: As soon as he found some other kids, or a car—or even a *bicycle*—he would find his own way to Mount Rainier and end the torture for good.

That night he dreamed of Julia Morrison.

They were back at his farm, at the Promised Land, and he was chasing her through the cornfields. Only it was a game, and they were both

56

laughing. "I'm going to get you!" he kept shouting, and she would shriek with delight. She wasn't pregnant or a heretic. She was just a *girl*—a beautiful, young girl, full of life and energy. And he was just a boy. They were together and alone: free from the shackles of their roles, free from the plague and the Visions and the Demon. They loved each other. . . .

His eyelids fluttered open.

The luminous warmth of the dream faded.

He rubbed his tired eyes, groaning—and rolled over in the darkness.

Damn. The sleeping bag was too hot, too tight. A gust of mountain wind chilled his exposed face. It was impossible to stay comfortable, to doze more than a few hours at a time. Why did Linda insist on camping out every night? They'd walked right past three hotels that very afternoon—hotels that were probably chock-full of beds. He fidgeted a few more times, then finally sat up straight. Enough of this nonsense. He was going to hike back down the road. The last hotel couldn't have been more than two hours away. He was going to sleep in a king-sized bed for twenty-four straight hours.

"Linda?" he barked.

She didn't answer.

He peered at her sleeping bag, lying on the other side of the smoldering remnants of their fire. It wasn't moving. She was sound asleep.

"Linda!" he yelled angrily. "Wake up!"

Not even a stir.

Seething, he wriggled free and stormed over to her. "Will you—"

He broke off in midsentence. *What on earth?* Linda's sleeping bag was empty. She was gone. He frowned and glanced around their campsite, squinting into the pitch black woods. Maybe she'd scampered off to relieve herself.

"Hey, Linda!" he shouted at the top of his lungs. "Where are you?"

But all he heard was the *dree-dree-dree* of the crickets.

Well. This was wonderful. *She* had left *him*. He had probably scared her away. After all his promises to himself, he still couldn't muster the courage to leave her. There had been plenty of chances, too. Several cars had sped past them that afternoon. He only needed to flag one down. But he still clung to that desperate, irrational hope that she would succumb to his will.

"Linda!" he screamed one last time.

Nothing.

So . . . it seemed as though there were three possible courses of action. He could sit around here and wait for Linda to return—which would be excruciating at best. Or he could search for her. That sounded like a fairly pointless activity as well. Or he could pack up his belongings and strike off on his own.

Why even bother to pack? It wasn't as if he needed his sleeping bag. From now on, he would be traveling first-class. He marched back around the fire, jammed his feet into his worn sneakers, and trotted out to the highway.

Remarkably enough, he felt awake, invigorated. Even *happy*. He was free, finally. If Linda was out of his sight, she would be out of his thoughts as well. No more obsession. No more unrequited longing.

The moon was very bright. His rubber soles slapped on the pavement in a steady rhythm. The road stretched before him, full of possibility. Maybe he'd track down part of his flock. A grin spread across his face. Maybe he'd even track down Larissa. . . .

He took a deep breath and surveyed the starry sky. Sweet Larissa. Where was she now? No doubt she was telling some other ripe teenagers about Harold's wondrous abilities—

What's that?

A red light was flashing on the eastern horizon.

He paused. *There*—three quick bursts: *blink-blink-blink*. His eyes zeroed in on a low mountaintop. After a brief pause the flashes appeared there again. Was it a satellite? A plane? No, it was stationary. Besides, planes and satellites didn't exist anymore. At least, he *guessed* they didn't.

Blink-blink-blink.

He frowned. Could it be a radio tower? Possibly. That would be encouraging. Maybe technology was being restored around here. Just in time for Harold to assume control.

The flashing stopped.

For a moment Harold hesitated. Oh, well. Whatever the message was, it was over. He shook his head and continued walking. Tomorrow he could try to find the source—

What the— A shadow was coming toward him down the road, staggering—weaving along like a drunk person . . . or somebody who was injured.

He held his breath. That couldn't be . . . but it was definitely a girl. A *tall* girl.

"Linda?" he called.

The shadow collapsed in a heap.

"Linda!" Terror seized him. He sprinted toward the girl, eyes wide, blood racing. *God, no.* It *was* Linda. Even in the darkness he could tell that she had been badly injured. Her clothes were in tatters. Her face was bruised, swollen beyond recognition. Hideous lacerations scarred her arms and legs. He bent beside her and tried to brush her hair off her forehead—but she scrambled away from him, rolling across the pavement.

"Stay away from me!" she screamed. "Don't touch me!"

Harold stumbled to his feet and held up his hands, palms outward. "Relax," he soothed. "I'm the Healer, remember? I just wanted to get a look at—"

"Just keep back," she whimpered. She crouched in a huddle, wrapping her arms around herself. Tears dripped from her cheeks. "Don't look at me."

Could this be . . . His mind immediately flashed back to medical school. *Assault.* He'd helped treat a battered woman during his first year as a resident. She'd exhibited the exact same behavior: a shrinking away from those trying to help her, an avoidance of eye contact. But who

60

could have possibly attacked her? He had to get a closer look. . . .

"The darkness is coming, Harold," she croaked. "The darkness."

He swallowed. "What darkness? Linda, you're in shock, okay? You—"

"No." She spun and thrust a finger at him. "The Demon did this to me, Harold. The Demon is everywhere, spreading darkness. And we better watch out."

**Babylon,
Washington
October 5-12**

October 5

I don't even know where to begin. So much crazy stuff happened while I was away. I can't believe it's only been a <u>month</u> since I left Babylon. It feels like a lifetime.

In a way, it <u>was</u> a lifetime. My brother's.

My feelings are being twisted and pulled in a hundred different directions. I always used to be so sure of things. People looked up to me. I was the chick who was in control and in charge. On second thought, scratch that. Until four days ago I was number one on America's most-wanted list. I honestly thought I was the Demon. It's so weird. It seems impossible to figure out what I went through or I'm going through now. But if I write things down, I can at least start to try to make sense of them.

That's what I'm hoping, anyway.

Maybe I'll start with the negatives. I'll get them out of the way. Then I can really focus on being Miz Positivity, like I've always planned. Sounds dorky, doesn't it? But I don't give a crap. From now on, I'm not going to concern myself with what anybody says or thinks about me anymore. I can take anything.

Almost anything.

Okay, maybe I'm getting ahead of myself. Maybe I'll just start with the negatives tomorrow.

October 6

So I'm trying to deal with the fact that Trevor is gone forever. But it's really, really hard. I cry a lot. I don't even know how it starts. The tears seem to come from nowhere.

That girl Sarah has been so cool about it. I guess I should call her the Chosen One. Somehow I just can't bring myself to say the words, though. She's so much more of a <u>Sarah</u>, a regular person, just like me.

I feel like we're bonding in this weird way, even though we're totally different. For one thing, there's the obvious fact that she's a messiah or whatever. She's sophisticated, too. She talks like a grown-up. I always thought that I had a pretty decent vocabulary until I met her. I guess she never watched a whole lot of TV. She doesn't get half my jokes. (Mental note: Maybe she <u>does</u> get them, and she just thinks they're lame?) And she went to college in Israel. How wild is that?

But she's really _nice._ I haven't been able to say that about anybody for a long time. Definitely none of my friends or ex-friends. She feels guilty for thinking I was the Demon, even though she doesn't even know me. It's amazing. She's the one who convinced everybody that I'm _not_ the Demon, but she still feels guilty.

I'm bummed I missed the day when she threw her magic scroll in a fire and walked on top of it. I've never seen anybody walk across hot coals before, not even on _The Guinness Book of World Records._ The whole thing sounds incredibly intense. Her whole _life_ sounds intense.

First she gets chased out of her home by Demon worshipers, then she finds a magical, three-thousand-year-old parchment that's full of prophecies and can't be destroyed. Then she's captured by an

Egyptian millionaire, and they almost
die, but they get rescued by this ocean
liner and sail to America, and they
fall in love, but

Oh, right. I was supposed to talk
about the negatives. Screw it. I'm too
tired.

October 7

I think I can finally say good-bye
to Trevor.

This afternoon Sarah and I carried
his body out and gave him a proper
burial in the back of WJS. I cried
again, but it was a relief. I couldn't
stand knowing that he was up there in
that classroom, lying around like a piece
of meat or something.

Sarah said some really nice things.
She said that even though he died
young, his life had been complete because
he helped save the world. She wasn't

exaggerating, either. Trevor helped rig up a radio system, and because of that, Sarah learned how to make the antidote for the plague. She also had a chance to talk one last time to her brother. Trevor made it happen.

She said Trevor was sorry for all the bad things he had done and that his heart was finally where it should have been all along. He said that he loved me and that he wanted to undo the past eleven years.

I figured I should say something, too, so I said that Trevor would be happy to be buried here. He loved this place. I couldn't really say much more because I couldn't talk.

Leslie wasn't there. She thinks a funeral was pointless for a creep like Trevor. I was pissed, but I kept my mouth shut. I think maybe she's jealous of my relationship with Sarah. She's been hanging out on the lawn with the rest of the kids, making new friends, being the proverbial social butterfly.

She still hasn't taken off the necklace. Nobody seems to be vaporizing, either. So what does that mean? Was her theory wrong? Has the necklace lost its power? Or was the whole thing in our heads? Maybe it never had any power in the first place. Maybe something else made me . . . invincible. I don't want to think about it.

October 9

Today, for the first time, I actually tried to mingle with people. _Tried_ being the key word.

Anyway, I walked right onto the lawn, right up to that big burning pot, right in front of all those kids. Leslie was pretty shocked. I guess she didn't think I would ever stop being a "wimp."

I can truthfully say, though, that I've never been more scared. I was shaking so badly, I could barely stand. I thought I would pee in my pants. I was sure somebody would vaporize, or attack me, or freak out, or something.

But nothing happened. Most people pretended that I wasn't there. It was like I had some awful disease. A couple of kids smiled, but their smiles looked really fake. Nobody would look me in the eye.

Maybe they all feel guilty, too, like Sarah. Most of them are still really bummed, of course. Jezebel is still out there, with the scroll. Somewhere.

I keep thinking about her. She used me. It's like I was violated or something. I was her best friend for ten years. Ten goddamn years. Well, maybe we weren't exactly friends, but we ran together. Was she planning to make me look like the Demon that whole time? I can't even describe how it makes me feel.

But Sarah says Jezebel might be an innocent victim. There's a chance that Jezebel doesn't even know what's happening to her. The Demon might have killed her spirit or soul or whatever you want to call it, then occupied her body.

I don't know if that makes me feel better or worse. It makes sense, though. Jez kept on saying that she wasn't Jezebel anymore. And Sarah told me one of the prophecies says that the Demon assumed a "human form" in April, possessing someone. That was when Jez flipped out. It all sounds too complicated to really understand.

Sarah has this notebook filled with stuff about the prophecies. She tried to show it to me, but it freaks me out too much. It's connected somehow with that feeling I have. The feeling that some terrible event is getting closer and closer. But I can't deal with it. I don't even know exactly what I'm afraid of.

I wonder where Jez is. I wonder where Caleb is, too. I wonder if he's still alive or if he ended up being another one of Jezebel's billions of victims.

October 12

Sarah just played me the most whacked-out thing I've ever heard in my life. It was this message, coming through Trevor's radio system. Some chick was jabbering about how the Chosen One is coming and that people should go to Mount Rainier to receive his blessing. She sounded like one of those late-night religious maniacs, the kind who tell you that the pyramids were built by aliens, then ask for money.

Sarah says it's some guy named Harold

who claims to be the Chosen One. He wants to get everyone in the same place, probably so he can kill them.

Then Leslie came bursting in, going on about how all the Chosen One freaks wanted to find Jezebel. I suggested that maybe she shouldn't call them "freaks" anymore, being as the Chosen One was right in front of her. Sarah got all embarrassed. But Leslie didn't even apologize. She acted as if Sarah wasn't even in the room. She's definitely jealous.

But I still love Leslie. I mean, she's my best friend. I'm just really sad and hurt and confused about Trevor. And I don't like to admit that kind of thing. I'm Miz Positivity.

One thing is for sure, though.

I'll never call anyone a Chosen One freak again.

**WIT Campus,
Babylon, Washington
Afternoon of October 13**

"It's like déjà vu," Sarah murmured, staring out the window at the noisy crowd. "I've seen this all before."

"What do you mean?" Ariel whispered.

Sarah sighed and slumped down into one of the hard wooden classroom chairs. "All those kids out there. . . . They're all shouting at each other, arguing about how they should deal with Jezebel. It's exactly what happened when I first came to Babylon. Except—" She couldn't bring herself to complete the thought. She didn't want to hurt Ariel's feelings or stir up painful memories. Not after all the suffering Ariel had just been through. . . .

"Except they were out to get *me*," Ariel finished. She cocked her eyebrow sympathetically. "It's all right, Sarah. I know all this stuff already. I'm cool with it. Really."

How? Sarah wondered. *How can you stay so cheerful and together all the time?* The girl was amazing. Ariel actually managed to *laugh* every once in a while. Sarah could barely bring herself to move, let alone smile. She felt as if a giant weight were slowly crushing her spirit. She'd lost her brother, the scroll . . . even her last friend: George Porter, the Visionary who ran off in search of his girlfriend.

But she couldn't start feeling sorry for herself. Not now. Compared to Ariel's problems, hers were almost insignificant. Ariel had lost *everything*. At least Sarah had a mob of believers on whom she could rely for support. And she might not have the scroll itself, but she still had a complete, word-for-word translation.

Although *that* hardly alleviated any stress or anguish. She almost wished Jezebel had stolen her notebook, too. Then she wouldn't know the truth: that the prophecies for this lunar cycle weren't being fulfilled.

For the first time ever, the three-thousand-year-old text seemed to be inaccurate.

And it terrified her.

Something is wrong. I'm not getting the whole picture. Or I made a mistake in the translation. It wouldn't be the first time—

"Hey, are you all right?" Ariel asked, leaning against the windowsill. "You seem really out of it."

"No, no, I'm fine," she lied. She forced a smile, then stared down at her long shadow on the dusty tile floor. "I'm just, uh, really impressed with how you're handling all of this. I wish I could say the same for me."

"Oh, yeah?" Ariel smirked. "Well, I'll let you in on a little secret. Inside, I'm totally freaking out. It's just that . . . well, I'm pretty good at hiding things. I've had a lot of practice. I spent all of high school pretending that I didn't care about jack." Her tone suddenly grew philosophical. "It's weird. I used to think that the less you showed people, the more they would like you. It was true, too, in a weird way. I mean, I was—"

"I've got to tell you something, Ariel," Sarah found herself saying.

Ariel's face turned bright red. "Oh, God, I—I'm sorry. . . ."

"No, I'm sorry," Sarah apologized. "I shouldn't have cut you off. But I have to talk about this with someone." She pushed herself out of the chair and scurried over to the worn backpack in the corner. "I'm really worried about the prophecies for this month. It says that I'm supposed to—"

"Hey, Sarah?" Ariel interrupted quietly. "I don't want to be rude or anything, but maybe you should talk about this with somebody else. I don't know if I'm the right person."

Sarah shook her head. "You're the perfect person, actually," she muttered, digging her coffee-stained red notebook out of the front pocket. "In a way, this has to do with you, too." She sat cross-legged on the floor and started flipping through her entries. "I mean, it sort of has to do with how I figured out that you *weren't* the Demon."

Ariel frowned. "I don't get it."

"You weren't fulfilling any of the prophecies," Sarah explained. "And Jezebel *was.*" She turned a few more of the weathered pages, then hopped up and strode back across the room. "Take a look at this." She held the notebook in front of Ariel and

77

pointed at two hastily scrawled lines from the ninth lunar cycle.

And the Demon will latch on to the Chosen One,
Following her incessantly, filling her head with lies

"See what I mean?" Sarah asked. "Jezebel was the one who latched on to me. She followed me around and lied to me. You weren't even in town. That's how I knew."

"Whoa." Ariel blinked at the words, slack jawed. "I still don't, um . . ."

Sarah quickly turned to the next section. "Anyway, part of the tenth lunar cycle says that Jezebel and I are going to fight, but neither of us will win. *That's* the part that worries me."

Ariel frowned. Her eyebrows were tightly knit. "Why?"

"Because it hasn't happened yet," she answered. "And it doesn't look like it's *going* to happen. I mean, how can I fight with Jezebel if she isn't here? There isn't much of a reason for her to come back, either. She has the scroll." Sarah nodded toward the notebook. "She has the 'key to the Future Time'—just like it says in here."

Ariel's eyes widened. Her face went pale. "So does that mean that Jezebel isn't . . ." She left the question hanging.

"No, I'm sure she's the Demon," Sarah soothed.

She patted Ariel on the shoulder. "I'm *positive*. I'm just not sure how to interpret this passage." She hesitated. A nervous twitter passed through her stomach. "I'm worried I might have copied it down wrong—"

"*There* you are!"

Sarah jerked in surprise.

Leslie stood in the doorway, panting. Her dark curls were in disarray. Her olive skin was damp, glistening in the sunlight. She shook her head and smiled. "I've been looking all over for you two," she gasped.

"Well, you found us," Ariel grumbled. "You also scared the crap out of me."

"Sorry, sorry." Leslie flopped down into a chair by the door, jangling her necklace. "But something just happened that might be really important."

Sarah took a deep breath and tossed the notebook onto the nearest desk. She tried her best not to appear irritated. "What is it?"

"This Chosen One freak named Bill just had this weird blackout and—"

"Jeez, Leslie," Ariel spat. "Why do you keep doing that?"

Leslie glared at her. "Doing *what*?"

Uh-oh. Sarah's eyes flashed between the two of them. Every time she'd seen them together lately, there had been major tension.

"You're calling that kid a 'freak' just to piss me off," Ariel snapped.

"Oh, *please*." Leslie groaned. "Look, it's a force of habit, all right? *You* were the one who started it, for

God's sake." She jerked a finger at Sarah. "Haven't you told *her* that your favorite pastime was ragging on COFs?"

Sarah stared at Leslie, baffled. "Coughs?"

Leslie gave her a brief, empty smile. "COFs. *C-O-F*s. Chosen One freaks."

"Oh," Sarah mumbled, feeling like an idiot. She lowered her gaze. Why did people always give her such a hard time? Why did they treat her as if she didn't have feelings? Or as if the kids who believed in her were either stupid or deluded? It wasn't as if she'd *asked* to be the Chosen One. . . .

"Let's just drop it, all right?" Ariel said. "We've been through this already. What's so important?"

"Well, this guy Bill had some kind of vision." Leslie's tone was cold and businesslike. "He said that the Demon is still *here*, in Babylon. Really nearby, in fact. But when somebody tried to ask him where exactly, he melted." She turned to Sarah. "What do you make of that?"

Sarah swallowed. She had no idea how to respond—or even what to think. Did that mean that the fight prophesied in the scroll *would* take place? But when? And how close was "nearby," anyway?

"Jezebel's probably hiding out and spying on us," Ariel muttered. "I bet she's picking the best time to attack."

"I wasn't asking *you*," Leslie snapped.

That's it. Sarah stepped forward. "Look, Leslie—I appreciate your telling me about this. But whatever is going on between you and Ariel . . . I just don't want to deal with it, all right? I have enough on my mind."

"Fine by me." Leslie shrugged and smiled again. She shot a quick glance at Ariel. "I don't want to deal with it, either. I want to help."

Ariel snorted, but she didn't say anything.

"Okay, then we have to figure out what to do," Sarah said. She pushed her glasses up the bridge of her nose and began pacing around the room. "And I guess we should probably start by trying to find Jezebel."

"*We?*" Leslie asked, raising her eyebrows. "I mean, I don't want to sound sour or anything, but how can Ariel and I help you? *You're* the Chosen One." She paused. "You're the one with the . . . you know, the powers."

Sarah gaped at her, astonished. "What powers?" she asked. "Have you ever seen me use any powers?"

Leslie bit her lip. "I . . . I—I didn't mean it in, like, you know, a bad way or anything," she stammered clumsily. Her eyes wandered to Ariel, then back to Sarah. "We just heard all about what you did—"

"It wasn't *me*, though," Sarah interrupted. "It was my scroll. *That's* what has the powers. I can't do a damn thing. I can't even crack the stupid code." The words seemed to stick in her throat. Her voice grew strained. "You want to know something else? The scroll says that I'm supposed to be even *weaker* this month. So excuse me if I ask for help, all right?"

Neither Leslie nor Ariel said a word.

Both of them stared at the floor.

What am I doing? Sarah wondered, glancing helplessly between the two girls. She was breathing too fast. *Why did I lose it? Why am I about to cry?*

She pulled her glasses off and wiped her moist eyes. It was pathetic. And frightening. She couldn't even control herself. So the prophecies were right about one thing, anyway. She was definitely weak. She was more than weak. She was falling apart.

"Well, here's what I think," Leslie whispered after a long silence. She stared down at her necklace and absently fiddled with it. "I think we should go find Jezebel and get that scroll back. Because if what you say is true, if *that's* what has the power . . . then Jezebel shouldn't have it."

Sarah nodded. Leslie was absolutely right, of course. She slipped her glasses back on, then glanced at Ariel. "What do you think?"

"I don't know," Ariel murmured. She shook her head, avoiding Sarah's eyes. "I think going after Jezebel is a mistake. Especially if you're—you know, weaker or whatever." She cleared her throat, stumbling awkwardly over the words. "Because even if you don't have powers or don't think you do, Jezebel *does*. We've seen what she can do. All of us."

"Well, we've seen what her necklace can do, anyway," Leslie muttered, fingering the pendant around her neck.

Sarah stared at her uncomprehendingly.

"That necklace belongs to the Demon," Ariel explained. "Leslie thinks it has powers or something. It's what kept me from dying when Jezebel stabbed me. It's the reason everyone thought I was the Demon."

"Hey! Maybe it's like the scroll is for you!" Leslie cried. "*You* don't have powers, but your scroll does. So maybe Jezebel doesn't have powers herself, either. Maybe only her necklace has powers."

Sarah shook her head, trying to clear it. This was getting way too confusing.

"So you *should* go find Jezebel—maybe she doesn't have any powers as long as we have the necklace," Leslie continued.

"Leslie, this is all just some big theory of yours," Ariel said in an annoyed tone. "You can't just send Sarah off to fight the Demon, *hoping* that you're right about all this."

"But then what about the scroll?" Sarah cried. The feeling of hopelessness expanded, consuming her. "What do we do about it? Do we just let Jezebel have it?"

Ariel nodded toward the notebook. "We still have the translation—"

"You're missing the point, Ariel," Leslie interrupted. "The point is the *power*. Just like Sarah said. And personally, I'm not too thrilled knowing that the Demon has all the power right now and the Chosen One has none. I think we should do something about it." Her lips pressed into a tight line. "It's worth the risk. I mean, she *is* the Chosen One."

"How can you say that?" Ariel's face grew red. "You're just trying to send Sarah away, aren't you?" she yelled. "You're jealous of her, and you're trying to get rid of her."

What? Sarah glanced at Ariel in surprise, but Ariel was staring at Leslie. *What is with these two? Aren't they supposed to be best friends?*

"You're crazy, Ariel!" Leslie cried. "Maybe this necklace ruined you permanently!"

"Maybe it's ruining *you!*" Ariel snapped. "Maybe that's why you're acting like a jealous bitch!"

"Oh, please." Leslie rolled her eyes. "What do I care about Sarah? I just want to stop the Demon, okay? And if *she* was any kind of a Chosen One, she'd *want* to fight the damn Demon! She wouldn't be afraid!"

Sarah winced. Leslie was right.

"How can you say things like that—," Ariel began.

"Why are you defending her?" Leslie cut in. "What do you *think* the Chosen One is supposed to do? She's supposed to save the world, isn't she?"

"She could get killed!" Ariel cried.

"Better her than everyone else on earth!" Leslie retorted.

Ariel's mouth fell open. "I can't believe you," she whispered. "Listen to yourself."

Leslie's dark eyes flashed with anger.

Quickly Sarah stepped between them. "Enough," she said, trying to sound in control. "I know what to do."

They both looked at her in surprise. "I will go find Jezebel—"

"Sarah, no!" Ariel interrupted.

Sarah held up her hand. "I will go. Soon. But I'll take the necklace with me."

"Excuse me?" Leslie said. "You're going to take an evil, powerful thing straight to the Demon?"

"Jezebel has my scroll and its powers. I'll have her necklace and its powers. We'll be even." Sarah couldn't believe how calm she sounded. "And if the necklace kept Ariel from being killed, maybe it will keep *me* safe, too."

"Oh, my God." Leslie laughed bitterly. "Don't you understand anything? The necklace kept Ariel from being killed because Jezebel *wanted* it that way. For all you know, if you put the necklace anywhere near her, she could just order it to make you melt."

"Yeah, or maybe the stupid necklace doesn't do anything," Ariel snapped. "Sarah, don't you see? We don't know anything about Jezebel or what she can do. It's just not safe for you to go."

Sarah sighed. Her head was spinning. "Well . . . why don't you give me the necklace anyway," she said. "If it kept Ariel safe, there's a chance it could keep me safe. It's my only hope." She held out her hand to Leslie.

Leslie just stared at her, openmouthed. She didn't move to take off the necklace.

"Give it to her, Leslie," Ariel said. "Or are *you* addicted to it now?"

Ariel's voice sounded odd, as if she were taunting Leslie. No matter how hard she tried, Sarah just couldn't understand these two.

"Fine!" Leslie spat. "Take the necklace right to the Demon and get us all killed!" She tore the chain off her neck and threw the pendant on the floor at Sarah's feet. "Happy now, Ariel?" she snarled. Then she whirled and stormed out of the room, slamming the door so hard that it rattled on its hinges.

My God.

Ariel burst into tears. She buried her face in her hands. "What's happening to us?" she wailed. "What's *happening?*"

Sarah sighed. *No, Ariel. Don't. It's going to be okay.* More than anything, she wanted to console her, to reach out . . . to make all of her pain disappear.

But she couldn't.

Because at that moment she started crying, too.

CHAPTER NINE

I'm standing in a cool, dark place . . . a cave, maybe. A fire is burning. I can feel the warmth of the flames on my skin. And next to the fire is a huge, old-fashioned hourglass—as tall as I am. The black sand inside is almost all gone. I stare at the falling grains, and I'm nervous. But I don't know why. It's that same feeling I always have: that something terrible is just over the horizon.

I know that it's something I can help prevent.

"We have to stop it," a voice whispers beside me.

It's a girl. I can't see who she is. She might be the Chosen One. I don't know. She's a friend, anyway. I'm sure of it.

"How?" I ask.

"I was hoping you could tell me," she says.

"I can't. But I feel like I'm closer now. I just need—"

"Hey, Ariel. Wake up."

A hand gently tapped Ariel's shoulder.

Her eyelids slowly opened. *Jeez.* It was so *bright.* She blinked a few times. Her face was mushed against a hard desktop, and her back was all bent out of shape.

"You were talking in your sleep."

Ariel sat up straight. Her mouth tasted like cotton. She glanced down at her closed journal . . . *right:* She'd wanted to write in it, but she must have passed out instead. It figured. She'd hardly slept in days. Sarah stood over her, smiling. She was wearing her backpack for some reason—and carrying her notebook. Bright sunlight streamed through the classroom windows, illuminating the pendant around Sarah's neck. Swirling motes of dust sparkled in the air.

"What were you dreaming?" Sarah asked.

"I, uh . . ." Ariel shook her head groggily. Her eyes narrowed. What *had* she been dreaming? The clarity of it seemed to melt away, like an ice cube under hot running water. Something about the Chosen One and an hourglass . . .

"I didn't mean to bother you," Sarah apologized.

"No, it's okay." Ariel squinted vacantly into space. "What was I saying?"

Sarah shrugged. "I couldn't really understand it." She laughed softly. "It sounded like nonsense. Or maybe you were talking in another language. It definitely wasn't English."

Another language? Ariel frowned. She didn't *know* other languages. Well, she'd taken a little Spanish in high school—but it was by far her worst subject. She hadn't learned a thing, other than *hola* and *gracias* and *hasta la vista, baby.* Weird.

"So, um . . . I came to say good-bye," Sarah said.

"Good-bye?" Ariel's head snapped up. "What do you mean?"

Sarah stared down at the notebook. "I'm going to find Jezebel now."

Ariel gasped. The sleepiness vanished. Fear and disbelief took its place. "B-but why?" she stammered. "We talked about this. You said you were gonna wait for her to come to you. You're safer here, remember? You know this place. You're surrounded by Visionaries. Everybody says that *this* is where they're being drawn to—"

"I changed my mind, Ariel," Sarah interrupted gently. "It's something I have to do. Jezebel isn't coming to me, so I have to go to her."

"But it doesn't make *sense,*" Ariel argued. She spoke in a desperate, frenzied rush. "It's too dangerous."

Sarah sighed and crouched beside her. "I know it's dangerous." She laid a hand on Ariel's arm and stared straight into her eyes. "But I've been thinking about this a lot. It's *all* I think about. And after going through every single argument in my mind a thousand times, I keep coming back to the same choice. I know you guys are mad at each other, but Leslie was right, Ariel. The longer Jezebel has the scroll, the worse it is for all of us—for *everybody.*" She glanced out the window. "And I'm willing to risk my life to get it back. Like Leslie said, it's worth the risk."

Ariel shook her head, horrified. "You can't listen to Leslie," she said in a trembling voice. "She doesn't care about you—she's only thinking of herself. She's jealous that we're friends; she thinks you're taking me away from her—"

"It doesn't matter," Sarah insisted. "Even if Leslie is being selfish, the *facts* are still the same. And what she said is absolutely true. All of the power is in Jezebel's hands."

Man. Sarah wasn't going to listen, was she? Despair descended over Ariel like a thick blanket. Sarah's decision had been made; her belongings had been packed. She had probably worn her backpack in here on purpose so that Ariel couldn't convince her to stay.

"And who knows?" Sarah continued. "Maybe there's nothing to be afraid of. Maybe the prophecies are right. They've never been wrong. Maybe I'll find Jezebel and fight with her, and neither of us will win. Or maybe the necklace will protect me. Or I *won't* find her. But I've got to try. Because I have a feeling . . . I don't know. Maybe *fighting* her is what it means to be the Chosen One, you know? To give everything, to risk everything, so that the Demon will be destroyed."

Ariel swallowed, gazing into Sarah's tired and re-signed eyes. *You don't really believe that the prophecies will come true, do you? You think something else will happen.* It was all right there, etched into Sarah's face: the grimness, the uncertainty. . . . She had no idea what she was facing. She was walking into the unknown. And she was terrified by it.

"You don't have to do this," Ariel pleaded one last time.

Sarah smiled sadly. "But I do." She stood up and

laid her notebook on Ariel's desk, then took a deep breath. "Anyway, I wanted you to have this. Just in case anything happens to me."

"What?" Ariel glanced up at Sarah, aghast. "Why would you give it to *me?*"

"Because if something *does* happen, I think you have the best shot at cracking the code."

For a second Ariel was almost tempted to laugh. "Are you crazy? There's no way—"

"Trevor was confident *he* could do it," Sarah stated, silencing Ariel in midsentence. "And you're his sister. Intelligence runs in your family. Anybody can see that."

Ariel slouched back in her chair. This was insane. "That's, uh . . . that's really flattering, but you don't know me so well, Sarah. Trevor and I were really different. He was born with the majority of the brains. I mean, he was a *genius*. I wasn't exactly in the running for school valedictorian." She shook her head. "I think you better find someone else."

Sarah's lips curled in a sad smile. "I don't *know* anyone else. And you're wrong. I think I know you pretty well. I mean, it's only been a few weeks, but even in this little bit of time, I saw something special in you. You give off this aura of . . . *positivity*. You can get things done."

The words stabbed into Ariel's chest. If only Sarah understood the irony of that statement. If only she knew how badly Ariel wanted it to be true. Sure, Ariel could get things done—but they were always bad, always malicious. She could never project any positive vibe. Because she would be constantly

91

haunted by the lies, the selfishness, the terrible games she had played with so many people . . .

"What's wrong?" Sarah asked.

Ariel felt her eyes fill with tears. She shifted her gaze to the sun-drenched window. "What's *right?*" she whispered. "That's a better question."

"What's right is that I'm giving you my journal," Sarah stated firmly. She placed her hand on the battered red cover. "Because hopefully the key to breaking the code is hidden somewhere in those pages." She paused for a moment. "One of the very last things my granduncle Elijah ever said to me was: 'Use the code.' I *know* it's the key to defeating the Demon. So in case I lose to Jezebel, it's up to you to find out how to win."

"But that's impossible," Ariel muttered, rubbing her eyes. She glanced back down at the notebook and bowed her head. "Where do I even start?"

Sarah patted Ariel's slumped shoulders. "At the beginning."

"What do you mean? Even if I—"

"Listen, I know it has something to do with the little passages of nonsense at the bottom of every fourth block of text," Sarah continued. "You'll see what I mean when you go through it. I wrote it all down. And both of our brothers said that it might have something to do with this thing called the Bible Code—where you take a letter in a sentence, then skip a certain number of letters, take another letter, skip the same number . . . and so on, until it spells out a message."

Great, Ariel thought wretchedly. *I couldn't even*

follow what you said. So how the hell am I supposed to do this?

"I think it might also have to do with the specific way I translated it," Sarah added. "But I'm not sure."

Ariel grabbed Sarah's arm. "This is a really, really bad idea, Sarah," she insisted. "All you did just now was confuse me. Don't you get it? I can't *do* this. So why don't you take off your backpack and stay here, and we'll work on it together until Jezebel comes around. . . ."

Her voice trailed off.

The bright morning sun had abruptly faded.

The classroom began to grow darker and darker, as if somebody were slowly dimming the lights. Ariel's fingers slipped from Sarah. The weather couldn't change *that* quickly. Her eyes flashed back to the window.

What the—

The sky . . . something was happening to it.

It looked as if it were being *covered.*

Only the clouds weren't puffy and white; they were black and terrifying—sweeping across the blue vault in a great billowing tidal wave.

Terror squeezed Ariel like a vise. It had to be a hallucination—she must have been drugged or something. *Jezebel.* Had Jezebel spiked the water at Edmunds Creek?

Screams drifted up from the lawn below.

"Sarah?" she whimpered.

"I see it," Sarah croaked.

"What . . . ?" Ariel couldn't complete the question.

She couldn't *speak*. All the blood seemed to flow from her body, leaving the pit of her stomach frozen and empty.

"Oh, my God!" Sarah shouted. "Today's the twenty-second, isn't it?"

The twenty-second?

"It's a sign, Ariel," she choked out. "It's a sign. I have to find Jezebel. I'll . . . I'll . . ." She turned and scrambled out the door.

"Sarah!" Ariel shrieked. "Come back here! Sarah, please! Don't . . ."

There was no answer. Before Ariel even finished screaming, Sarah's footsteps had faded.

I must still be asleep, Ariel thought. Her lungs heaved. She twisted one way, then another, but still couldn't manage to get out of her seat. *It's a nightmare. I only imagined I woke up. It's too senseless, too strange. . . .*

But the sudden darkness didn't even terrify her the most.

No. What terrified her more than anything was the certain knowledge that she would never see Sarah alive again.

PART III:

October 23-31

The Tenth Lunar Cycle

Anticipation surged through Naamah like a river of molten lava.

Very little time remained. The moon would only circle the earth once more before Lilith revealed herself . . . only twice more before the ancient weapon exploded in fury.

And after those two final cycles, the moons would be moons of victory—shining down upon the earth for all eternity.

Still, hidden surprises lurked around every corner, as Naamah had just recently discovered.

Harold Wurf's lust was a perfect example. In all of Naamah's careful planning, in all the many scenarios she had considered, she had never imagined that Harold's sexual frustration would actually tempt him to leave her. She'd never realized the potential danger.

Yet now—looking at the incident in retrospect—it seemed obvious . . . perhaps inevitable.

She'd flirted with him too heavily. She'd also

underestimated his sense of entitlement. Once again her overconfidence proved to be a weakness. She had forgotten the totality of her role as Linda Altman. Because in spite of her obvious beauty and intellectual superiority, she was still supposed to be a member of Harold's flock—a servant, a lackey.

No follower had refused Harold's transparent charms before. Most of the girls in his flock were infatuated with him. And perhaps since Naamah found that adoration so distasteful, she hadn't bothered to examine how it affected him. Indeed, she had dismissed him as a sexist egomaniac—knowing that his was a dying breed.

Pitiful boys like Harold would have no place in the New Era. Lilith was embarking on an age of female dominance . . . where Naamah and the other high priestesses would reign with an iron fist.

And in the end, another shrewd performance on Naamah's part solved the problem. Linda Altman's "injuries" quashed Harold's desire like a wrecking ball. He could no longer stand the sight of her ruined face. And since she cried out every time he drew close, he would never learn that the scars and bruises were false: a meticulously applied coat of theatrical makeup and putty.

She had turned his attraction into revulsion.

But the Demon's mythical "attack" had accomplished much more than that. It had struck fear deep into Harold's soul. Now cowardice prevented him from leaving her. He was afraid that the Demon would seek her out again, perhaps even kill her—and that he would be left all alone, without her visions to guide him.

And when the Darkness obliterated the sun on October 22, Harold's fear turned to terror.

For it proved that the Demon was indeed everywhere. And the Demon was cunning. The Demon could assume a human face and hide in a crowd. The Demon could fool Harold and Naamah into splitting up. So they had to avoid any contact with other people. They had to stick to the lonely trails and side roads. Naamah swore that the Demon couldn't hurt her so long as Harold remained at her side during the dark days. She swore that the Demon would be powerless in his presence. She swore that the attack was her fault—because she had left their campsite to wander off in the middle of the night, down that lonely highway, without Harold's protection. . . .

They had to stay together, out of sight, until they reached Mount Rainier.

It was a brilliant ruse for the truth.

Naamah simply had to keep Harold isolated to prevent him from discovering the existence of the plague's antidote.

Yes . . . the antidote was proving to be a greater problem than expected. Her fellow Lilum had failed to destroy the Russian base at Strizhi before the recipe was broadcast around the globe. Now the secret was spreading from Babylon and other places in ever-growing concentric circles, like ripples in a pond. The mishap was infuriating, but it also served as a potent warning. Despite Lilith's advantages, Naamah and her sisters still had a few obstacles to overcome in ensuring their victory.

If Harold learned of the antidote, he might start to doubt his own legitimacy.

Why would the survivors need a savior if they could stay alive by doing something as trivial as swallowing a specially prepared turnip bulb?

No . . . she couldn't risk his finding out. He might grow angry. He might not be able to fulfill his final task for Lilith. Indeed, he might even come to suspect that he had been manipulated. He was smart; she had to acknowledge that. It was the only way she could control him. She could never doubt his insight or intelligence. So she would shelter him while his flock continued to spread the word of his imminent blessing.

And as for the people who had already taken the antidote, the people who would not heed the command to assemble at Mount Rainier . . . they would also meet with their destinies.

Lilith had a plan for them as well.

CHAPTER
TEN

I'm starting over today. Again. This new diary makes it official. I found it in karen's bedroom. She was the youngest. I learned all of their names. karen, Marijke, and Johann Smit. I feel like a Smit myself. I know this family as well as I ever knew my own. I've lived in their mansion for three weeks. I've eaten their food and slept in every single bed. I've read their books and gone through their stuff and worn their clothes.

I wonder why karen never used this diary. Maybe she got it as a Christmas present right before the plague and she forgot about it. I'm glad she did. The pages are smooth and blank and

103

brand-new. A clean slate. I'm a new person, with a new life. And it's a life as alien to me as that of a stranger.

But that's hardly a new sensation. I've felt the same exact way a lot of times since New Year's Eve, in a lot of different places and under a lot of different circumstances. The difference is that this time, I'm okay with it. I'm going to stop looking for answers. I'm just going to let things _happen_. I'm not going to make any judgments, either. It's the only way I'll stay sane and healthy. It's the only way my baby will survive.

I'm doing it for her.

Two days have gone by, and it's still as dark as night outside. Maybe it will stay that way forever. Maybe I'll never see the sun or the moon or the stars again.

I don't mind it so much, though. Because the black cloud taught me something. It taught me that my visions are connected to the sun in some way. I don't know how, of course. I don't care, either. All I know is that I don't pass out and dream about the Chosen One anymore. I don't feel the pull. I don't even know which way is west.

I feel like a prisoner who's been pardoned. The awful, unknown burden has been lifted. I'm not compelled to keep moving, to try to stop some terrible thing that's going to happen very soon.

I can just <u>live.</u>

I remember feeling this way back in March. I stopped having visions then, too. Most of all, though, I remember being happy. George and I lived in that little cabin, that little self-contained world. The rain poured outside, all day and all night. Our partnership blossomed into love. It was the most powerful thing I ever felt or ever will.

But I'm going to channel all that love into our baby. I'm going to follow our own example and turn this mansion into the same little self-contained world for my baby and me. I know we can survive here. There's lots of food and farmland.

And for some reason, I see myself getting old. My baby, too. Maybe it's just wishful thinking, but I feel like this cloud marks the end of everything. The end of the plague. The end of the Chosen One. It could be that the Demon won, but I

Julia dropped her pen.
The doorbell was ringing.
Dingdong . . . dingdong . . .
How was that possible?
She sat rigid as a statue in the warm glow of the desk lamp. It had to be the wind. Or maybe the doorbell was broken. Because she was all alone. Not a soul had stirred in this dead town in three whole weeks. And that was the way she liked it. The solitude was very reassuring, very safe. She didn't *want* to see or talk to anyone, especially since she was s

groggy and uncomfortable most of the time. Her belly seemed to swell another inch every day—

Dingdong . . .

A twitter of anxiety passed through her. She should probably go downstairs and take a look. Even if people *were* there, they were probably perfectly friendly. Maybe they were neighbors. Or family. More Smits. She'd like that. Harold couldn't have been able to track her down. Not to this remote, forgotten place. He probably thought she was dead. Besides, how could anybody find their way *anywhere* in this darkness?

Dingdong—

"Coming!" she found herself yelling.

With a grunt she pushed back the chair and forced herself to stand. She was so *heavy*. How could an unborn baby weigh her down so much? She planted her hands on her hips for support, then carefully plodded out into the hall—down the sweeping stairwell to the checkerboard marble foyer. Every footstep sent a jolt of pain through her spine. *Less than two months,* she reminded herself. *Probably only six more weeks . . .*

"Hello?" a boy yelled outside the door. "Anybody home?"

Julia paused at the peephole.

"Who is it?" she called. But why was she even asking? Aside from Harold and his followers, every single human being left on earth was a stranger.

"My name's Ted," the voice answered. He sounded surprisingly upbeat—almost cheerful. "Me and my buddy Bob were driving by, and we noticed that some of the lights were on. Is it cool if we come in?"

"Um . . ." Julia leaned forward and squinted through the tiny glass. But she couldn't see a thing. It was too dark. The restless nervousness was returning. "What do you want?"

The boy laughed. "Well, for one thing, I'm really lost. I'm trying to get back to Chicago. This cloud cover has kinda screwed me up. I was hoping you might have a map."

Cloud cover? Julia drew back her head. That was a pretty benign phrase for the inexplicable, evil black mist. . . .

"We're kind of hungry, too," another boy chimed in.

Julia stood there, shifting on her feet. She supposed she could just tell them to go away. But what if they *were* hungry? She knew a lot about hunger, *real* hunger: the kind that invaded your body and drove everything out except pain and the necessity to end it. Maybe she should help them. On the other hand, they couldn't be *that* famished. A starving person wouldn't laugh or make polite chitchat. The silent seconds ticked by with dreadful slowness. She should have stayed upstairs. Now she had to make a decision—

"Hey, we don't mean to bother you," the first guy said. "If you could just tell us how to get back on the highway, that would be great."

"No, no." Julia shook her head. She took a deep breath, then unlatched the door and pulled it open. "Come in."

Two boys strolled into the hall. Both were wearing yellow raincoats. They looked surprisingly healthy and well kempt. Neither exuded the typical, depressed listlessness that most kids did these days. There was color in their cheeks; they were *clean*. One had a buzz cut. The other had long black hair, parted in the middle.

"I'm Ted," said the long-haired guy.

"I'm Bob," said the other.

Julia closed the door slowly, scrutinizing their faces. *Ted and Bob.* Was it her imagination, or had she met these guys before? They definitely weren't part of Harold's flock. No, she had memorized every follower's face, every name. Had they gone to her high school? Possibly. But what would they be doing all the way out here, in Idaho of all places? They *were* familiar, though. Those raincoats . . .

And then she noticed something.

They were staring at her as well.

"Don't I . . . ?" they both began at the same time.

Julia's eyes narrowed. "Yeah," she murmured.

A tentative smile spread across Ted's face. "You know what it is? I think we met you on the road once. You and some guy . . ." He blinked a few times, nodding. "It was in that flood outside Springfield, back in March. That's it. I remember now. I think we really freaked you out. You got into our car, then ran away. It was like you saw a ghost or something."

That's right! The memory was so clear now: She and George *had* met these guys. She and George had climbed into their Range Rover in the middle of a downpour—and then those two started talking about the Chosen One. Julia had immediately assumed they were with those evil girls from Ohio. . . .

Bob chuckled. "What are the chances of *that,* huh?"

That was a very good question. What *were* the chances? Very small. Insignificant. In fact, it was totally unlikely that she would have run into these boys again—unless there was a reason. Unless they were connected to the Demon in some way . . .

Julia's heart skipped a beat. She glanced from one to the other. But they were just gazing at her with those same vacant smiles.

"Hey, you're pregnant!" Ted suddenly cried, pointing at her stomach. "Congratulations!"

She swallowed. Now she was scared. Nobody had ever congratulated her for being pregnant before. Harold had tried to *kill* her for it. And it was a fairly inappropriate comment since everybody under the age of fifteen had long since vaporized. Any reasonable person could assume that the baby would be doomed—destined to turn into a puddle of black slime at the moment of birth. Unless . . .

Maybe these guys were Visionaries, like the Smit siblings.

Maybe they knew something about her baby that she didn't.

"Looks like you're due any day now," Ted commented breezily. His eyes wandered up the stairs. "It's funny. Somebody told us we were gonna run into a pregnant girl. Say, where's the lucky father? Is he around?"

"He's, uh . . . he's dead," Julia whispered, backing away from them.

Ted's smile vanished. He exchanged a quick glance with Bob, then lowered his eyes. "Hey, I'm really sorry," he murmured. "I didn't mean . . ."

"Look, we'll just be on our way," Bob muttered sheepishly.

Good. Julia's hands covered her stomach. Her palms were moist. Who could have told them that they would run into a pregnant girl? Nobody knew she was here. *Nobody.*

Bob turned to the door, then hesitated. "You don't happen to have any spare bulbs—"

"Hey!" Ted barked, scowling. "What's your problem? *She* needs them more than we do."

Julia stared at them uncomprehendingly.

Ted and Bob exchanged another glance.

"What are you talking about?" Julia demanded. She was sick of this. She wanted answers. "What *bulbs?*"

"How long have you been here?" Ted suddenly asked. His tone was sharp, probing.

"None of your business," Julia spat.

"But have you been to Babylon?" he pressed. "Do you know about Babylon?"

Babylon. Julia blinked. That was a place in the Bible, wasn't it? Could it be that these guys were Fundamentalist Christians? It would explain why they had been looking for the Chosen One back in March. Maybe they thought that the Chosen One had something to do with the Second Coming. It would make sense, wouldn't it? A lot of other kids probably thought the same thing. *That* would be a relief. Maybe they *weren't* dangerous.

Ted sighed. "You don't know, do you? You don't know anything."

"Apparently not," she answered carefully.

"We found the Chosen One," he proclaimed. "She's in this little suburb of Seattle. A town called Babylon. She sailed across the sea from Jerusalem to deliver the cure for the plague."

"What?" Julia cried.

Ted looked at Bob, and the two of them started smiling.

"The cure comes in these turnip bulbs," Bob explained. "I just figured you knew about it. Everybody else does. See, the Chosen One's helper gave us the recipe for making it, but we don't have any on us. And, you know, I just wanted to know if you had any extra because my twenty-first birthday is coming up, so—"

"You've *seen* the Chosen One?" Julia demanded, cutting him off.

"Uh . . . yeah," Bob mumbled. "We met her. Her name's Sarah."

The Chosen One. Julia's mind raced in a thousand different directions. She just couldn't bring herself to accept it: The Chosen One was real, here, alive . . . curing people. Maybe Julia should go try to find her. Washington wasn't that far from Idaho, was it? If she got there before her baby was born, then her baby would be sure to survive. But what about the Demon? What about her visions? Had she stopped having them because the Chosen One had already won the battle? But she still didn't even know if she could *trust* these guys. . . .

"Look, we can take you back there if you want," Ted offered.

Julia frowned at him. "I thought you wanted to

go to Chicago."

He shrugged. "It's no big deal. I mean, a couple more weeks on the road isn't gonna kill us." He nodded toward Julia's bulging midsection. "Anyway, I'm not just gonna leave you stranded here like that. You're gonna have a baby. You need to see Sarah. We can go back."

"Why did you guys leave, anyway?" Julia asked. "Didn't you want to stay?"

He shook his head. "Things are kind of weird up there." He scratched his nose, fidgeting, hesitating. "See, the Demon's there too—"

"*What?*" Julia shrieked. She gripped her stomach again. "Oh, my God . . ."

Ted nodded grimly. "Yeah, and everybody's freaking out. The black cloud didn't do much to make us feel better. That's why we left. See, the Demon is hiding. All the Visionaries still think that something really bad is gonna happen. . . ." He glanced at Bob.

Bob was staring at him. "Are you thinking—"

"Yeah." Ted nodded again. "I am."

"Thinking what?" Julia demanded, fighting back another surge of fear. "What are you talking about?"

Ted took a deep breath. "This guy . . . the one who told us we'd run into a pregnant girl? He said that the baby was special. He said that the baby was gonna help destroy the Demon."

Good Lord. Karen Smit's words whirled through Julia's mind: "*We know about your daughter. She's the child of the Blessed Visionaries. The Chosen One will anoint her as her heir. Your daughter will lead those who defeat the Demon into a glorious*

113

New Era."

No . . . it couldn't be true. There was no way some-body like *her* could give birth to somebody like *that*. She wasn't blessed. She was weak and helpless and alone. . . .

"I think we better take you to Babylon," Ted said. "I don't think we even have a choice."

Julia gaped at them.

So the battle wasn't over. It was still raging. And her burden would never be lifted. It *wasn't* a coinci-dence that these guys had found her. It was an omen: a sign that she could never run away or escape the terrible duty for which she had been chosen.

Ted was right. They didn't have a choice. And nei-ther did she.

Old Pine Mall,
Babylon, Washington
Night of October 26

"I think that's the last of it," Jezebel muttered.

Caleb struggled to sit up straight. But he kept sliding down—deeper and deeper into the plastic kiddie pool. Better just to lie on his butt. *Mmmm.* Nice and soft. One of these days, they were going to have to fill this thing with water. *Hot* water. And bubble bath mix. Yeah. This toy store had to be stocked with that kind of stuff, right? That would be so cool. . . .

"Shoot," she hissed. "I gotta get some more."

Jezebel was beside him, holding the dark bottle of peppermint schnapps upside down and shaking it. But he kept seeing two of her. Every time he blinked, they would spin to the right. *Stop it.* Why was she moving? She wasn't doing a whole lot to help put out the queasy fire in his belly. Maybe he was more wasted than he thought. Maybe he should just close his eyes. It was too much of an effort to keep them open, anyway—

"Hey!" he yelped.

The tub squeaked loudly and shimmied, then tossed him on his side. He flung out his hands to

115

balance himself. Jezebel was scrambling to her feet. *Damn, girl, what's your problem?* Her body swirled in the candlelight—then vanished down the action figure aisle.

"Wai-uh-mih!" Caleb protested.

But she was gone, lost in the darkness of a thousand Barbie dolls and Power Ranger action figures. He frowned. Why couldn't he speak? The thought was there: *Wait a minute.* The problem was that his lips were too rubbery and his tongue was too dry. He needed more booze to lubricate the vocal mechanism. And to quench his thirst. *Cheers!* He giggled once, then hiccuped.

"I'll be right back," Jezebel called. Her voice was very far away. "There's another stash in the food court. . . ."

Caleb shook his head. "I'm comin' too," he slurred. "So jus' . . ." *Forget it.* It was way too hard to say the words. He needed to put all of his energy into getting himself out of this tub and onto his feet. But Jezebel had knocked him all out of whack. He flopped around for a few seconds, trying to get his bearings—then gave up. His eyelids grew heavy again. Why did everything have to be so *hard?*

Uh-oh.

Did he have to pee?

Nah . . . he could wait. After the next drink. He rolled over on his back again. *Wow.* The ceiling looked really intense in the candles—all trippy and shadowy. Little flecks of orange light danced across the room. His arms and legs dangled loosely over the

116

side of the pool. A crooked grin crossed his face. Hopefully those rusted lighting fixtures wouldn't fall on him or anything. . . .

Now there's an idea.

Could he rig them so that they would fall on Jezebel?

That would be *perfect*, actually. He couldn't do it now, of course. But once he sobered up, he would find a way to distract her so he could loosen the wiring. Maybe he could even connect some kind of lever—a string he could tug to release the lights at exactly the right moment. *Bam!* It would knock her right out. He laughed. That would be awesome. Those things *had* to be heavy, right? They were at least four feet long. They probably wouldn't kill her, but he could finish that job himself.

Tomorrow. Yeah. No more putting things off. He'd wasted enough time in this hellhole. When was the last time he'd gone outside—or even seen the light of day? Not for a week, at least. Jezebel kept him stuffed with snacks she whipped up at the food court, so he didn't even have to go anywhere to feed himself. His meals were made to order. Breakfast in bed: morning, noon, and night. One greasy bowl of burnt french fries? Yes, sirree! Coming up! And served with a smile, no less! The only time he even left the toy store was to relieve himself in the men's room down the hall. Always at night, too. The mall was always dark.

"Jezebel!" he barked.

He allowed himself a little smile. He *could* speak.

She didn't answer, though. Maybe she'd gone to

the bathroom or something. It certainly didn't take *this* long to run to the food court and back—not that he had any idea of how long she'd been gone. He'd totally lost any concept of time in this place. For all he knew, it could be either 4 A.M. or 4 P.M. It really didn't matter, though—

Here she comes.

Footsteps crept down the aisle.

Only . . . those footsteps didn't belong to Jezebel. He frowned. No. He knew the way Jezebel walked. It wasn't nearly so soft and catlike. How drunk was he, anyway? With a savage effort he dug his palms into plastic and forced himself into a semblance of an upright sitting position.

Somebody stepped into the candlelight. His pulse instantly doubled.

It *wasn't* her. It was a girl: tall and beautiful, dressed in a short black miniskirt—a girl he hadn't seen in over two months. . . .

"Leslie?" he gasped.

She stopped at the foot of the pool. Her eyes widened. Her hands flew up to her face. "Oh, my God, Caleb, what has she *done* to you?"

He blinked at her, openmouthed. "Uh . . . what do you mean?"

"You look terrible!" she cried.

I do? That sure killed his buzz. Now he was just annoyed. Leslie had no business being in here. She'd screw up his plan—

"Are you okay?" she whispered, crouching beside him. She reached out and touched his arm. "You seem really out of it. What did she—"

"I've been drinking peppermint schnapps," he interrupted. "With Jezebel." His words were slower than usual, but still, they were very crisp and clear. *Good.* He'd gotten a grip on himself. He was in control. "She's on her way back. So you better get out of here . . ." He paused.

Leslie was shaking her head violently.

"What?" he demanded.

"I just saw her running out the door," Leslie whispered.

Caleb rolled his eyes. "Get outta here."

"I'm *serious.* She was carrying a gun, Caleb. A pistol. Probably the same one she killed Trevor with. Don't you understand? This is *bad."*

"Oh, come on." Caleb groaned. "She's in the food court, getting me booze." He glared at her. But the old, mischievous sparkle was nowhere to be found. He swallowed, suddenly very nervous. "You're not kidding?"

"No," Leslie stated. "And the thing is, I can't find anybody." She let his arm go and stood, glancing back down the aisle. "I've been looking all over for Sarah and Ariel. They're gone."

Ariel! At the mention of her name his chest tightened, as if the air had been sucked out of his lungs. "Is—is Ariel really back in town?" he stammered.

Leslie turned to him. "She's been back for four weeks." Her voice was hollow. "She and Sarah are, like, best friends now."

Best friends? He tried to force a shaky smile. "Wow. That's great, isn't it? I mean, if the Chosen

119

One likes Ariel, then everyone must finally know they were wrong about her, right?"

"Yeah, everybody *does* know," Leslie barked. Her expression hardened. "Everybody knows that Jezebel is the Demon. Which brings me back to my first question. What has she *done* to you? Why are you here?"

Caleb averted his eyes. He opened his mouth, then closed it. He couldn't tell Leslie why he was here; it was too great a risk. Nobody could know of his plan. If somebody else found out, then Jezebel might discover the truth as well.

"I can't say," he finally murmured.

"You *can't?* Or you *won't?*" Leslie's voice rose to a shout. "This isn't a game, Caleb. Sarah went to look for Jezebel. Ariel probably went after her. Why do you think Jezebel turned the sky black? She probably wants to sneak up on them and kill them both at the same time—"

"What do you mean, turned the sky black?" Caleb interrupted. She jabbed a finger toward the door. "Go take a look outside, Caleb!" she screamed. The veins in her neck turned bright red. They looked as if they might burst. "The sky isn't blue anymore. It's *black*. The sun hasn't been out in over four days."

Oh, man . . . His stomach seemed to catch fire again—and this time he was certain he would be sick. So now he knew why the hall was always so dark. He didn't only have to pee at night, did he? No. Daylight had disappeared *outside* these walls, too. He should have known some terrible catastrophe would happen again. It was just like the time Jezebel made it rain blood. No wonder she had been so pleased with herself recently. . . .

"Go on," Leslie commanded.

He shook his head. "I—I'll take your word for it," he managed.

"So *answer* me, Caleb. Why are you here?"

Caleb stared back at her. Maybe he should confess. If what she was saying was true, then he probably had nothing to lose. Because if Jezebel had ditched him to hunt down Sarah and Ariel, then his plan had failed. She wasn't any weaker. *He* was. He was the drunk who was sprawled in the kiddie pool—and she was the murderer who had turned the sky black. Had he really expected to succeed? He'd been a fool to think he was any kind of match for her. No, he was a certified, card-carrying *idiot*.

"I'm waiting," Leslie growled.

He hung his head. "I was trying to kill her," he admitted wretchedly. "I wanted her to trust me. So I stayed here with her day after day, hoping to catch her off guard . . ." He couldn't go on. It was too depressing.

And then, much to his surprise, Leslie crawled into the tub beside him.

"Caleb, I'm sorry," she said. "I should have known."

He swallowed. His throat was clogged. "I was doing it for Ariel," he whispered.

"I know. I came here for Ariel, too."

Caleb glanced at her. Her eyes were very close to his own. He couldn't believe it: They were red and brimming with tears. Leslie Tisch was actually *crying*.

"What do you mean?" he asked.

"I've been such a bitch," she said tremulously. She sniffed loudly and tossed her black curls over her shoulder, obviously fighting to compose herself. "We had a really big fight because of the Chosen One . . . and Ariel thinks it's because of the necklace. . . ."

"Necklace?" Caleb repeated.

Leslie shook her head. "It would take too long to explain. The thing is, I don't want to fight with her. We never fought before we came back here. She's my . . . she's my best friend. I haven't talked to her since our fight. I went to her house and looked for her, and she wasn't there, and she wasn't at WIT, either, and I got so freaked out—"

"Shhh," Caleb soothed. He draped his arm around her shoulders. "It'll be okay. She'll understand. She's good at forgiving people, you know?"

"But what if I don't find her?" Leslie sobbed, leaning against him.

"You *will,*" Caleb promised. "I know it. She's too smart for Jezebel. Besides, she's with Sarah, right?"

"I hope so." Leslie rubbed her eyes. She shook her head and chuckled sadly.

"What is it?"

"Nothing." She sighed. "I've just been, ah . . . I've been thinking a lot about different things lately. And I realized something. I'm a bad person. I never thought of myself that way."

Caleb ran a hand through her hair. It was so

122

weird: Jezebel had said the exact same thing. And compared to Jezebel . . . But there *was* no comparison. "You're not bad."

"I'm not?" Her lips quivered. "I really yelled at Ariel—I said the stupid necklace had damaged her somehow. I didn't even mean it, but I said it. I . . . I . . ."

"But you saved her *life,*" Caleb reminded her. "Remember? And you were the one who always believed in her, right from the very beginning. That's more than anybody else can say. Including me." The terrible, gnawing guilt invaded him again. It tore at his insides. "You're not a bad person. There's no such thing. *Everybody's* a little bad. Everybody's a little good, too."

A tear fell from her cheek. "But I want to find her so badly," she wept. "I want to go to her house so we can just forget about stuff and laugh. I want to look through *Skintight* with her again. Remember that cheesy porn book, with all the pictures from those X-rated seventies flicks?" She laughed through her tears. "You and I looked at it together, remember? In a tub, too. Like this one. Only nicer."

Caleb nodded. He tried to smile but couldn't. The lump in his throat expanded. How could he ever forget that day? He'd felt as though he and Leslie were the only two people on earth . . . as if everyone else had simply ceased to exist.

Just the way I feel now, he realized.

Only now, for all he knew, it might be *true.*

Leslie turned to face him. For a long while he gazed back into her sad, dark, dreamy eyes . . . then

123

leaned over and kissed her on the lips. And she kissed him back. But there was nothing fervent or sexual about it. No, it was *tender*—motivated, more than anything, by the simple need to connect with another human being.

It was a connection Caleb hadn't felt in a very, very long time.

187 Puget Drive,
Babylon, Washington
Morning of October 27

When Sarah first tiptoed into the front hall, she knew she wasn't alone.

She couldn't explain it. The front door was wide open, of course, but plenty of doors were open on this street. And from what she could tell, the houses were all empty. It was just a *feeling*—an intangible hunch that somebody else was here. She pulled a flashlight from her backpack and clicked it on, waving the bright beam of light through the living room.

It's like a museum, she thought with an odd chill. *A monument to the past.* The place literally looked as if it had been frozen in time on New Year's Eve. Beer bottles littered the worn rug. The glass coffee table was stained with dark rings. Couch pillows were strewn haphazardly in front of the dust-covered television set. . . .

The back of her neck tingled.

Is Jezebel watching me right now? Or am I imagining things?

Reason would seem to indicate that the dark, silent house was deserted. The old Sarah Levy would have scoffed at her "premonition"—blaming

125

it on exhaustion and an overactive brain. Nobody was here. Besides, it was impossible to tell if she was being watched just from a little prickle in her spine.

Wasn't it?

She swung the flashlight toward the carpeted stairwell.

That, too, was empty.

A tired sigh escaped her lips. What was she *doing?* Five days had passed—five days of incessant, fearful wandering under that black sky—and Sarah hadn't found Jezebel or even a *trace* of her. Maybe Ariel was right. Maybe Jezebel would find them at WIT. Besides, Jezebel wouldn't hide out in Ariel's house, would she? She *hated* Ariel. This would be the last place she'd seek refuge.

Yet even as Sarah argued with herself, she knew the only reason she had bothered coming here was precisely *because* it was so unlikely. And Jezebel was very smart. She saw what others were thinking and turned those thoughts against them. . . .

The tingle grew stronger.

Sarah swallowed. Why didn't *she* have the power to read a person's mind? This necklace didn't seem to be giving her any special powers. It wasn't fair. Jezebel was so much stronger than she was. *Everybody* was. Everybody she had ever met was so sure of themselves—especially the Visionaries. Like George. He was always certain of what needed to be done. He *had* to come to Babylon. He *had* to find his girlfriend. He never second-guessed himself. Ibrahim had been that way, too. They had tasks, missions—a *purpose.* So why was *she* plagued with insecurity and self-doubt?

Maybe it was her punishment for a lifetime of cynicism. She could never have faith in herself because she'd never had faith in anything else. At least, not until very recently. Not in the existence of God, not in the psychic abilities of human beings . . . Before she found the scroll, she wouldn't believe in anything she couldn't see with her own eyes.

And even after she verified the truth of the prophecies, she *still* found it almost impossible to accept that she had been picked at random three thousand years ago to battle the Demon.

Why me?

That was the question—the *only* question.

But did the answer even matter?

The fact remained that she *had* been chosen. So she *did* have a purpose. And that purpose was very clear. She had to destroy the Demon. For good. Forever. It was the only thing she could do. She couldn't crack the code; she couldn't discover whatever it was Elijah had wanted her to do. But she could stop the Demon. And that's what she would do. Because in spite of what she told Ariel, she didn't merely intend to retrieve the scroll. She intended to put a bullet into Jezebel's heart.

I'm going to kill her. I'm going to put an end to the countdown. I'm going to prevent the terrible thing that awaits us all at the end of the twelfth lunar cycle—whatever it may be. If the Demon is dead, the prophecies can't be fulfilled. The human race will triumph. I'm going to kill her.

A momentary tremor rattled Sarah's bones as she thought of the pistol tucked into her pants. The cold metal pressed against the small of her back. Nobody knew she had found Trevor's secret cache of weapons. It was a secret. And even when she swiped one of the guns, she wasn't sure if she could ever use it. She'd never pulled a trigger before in her life. But if she stuck to her resolve, if she summoned the courage . . .

A door slammed upstairs.

Sarah flinched.

"Hey. Who's down there?"

Jezebel?

She couldn't believe it. A bitter queasiness rose in her gut. The hunch was *right*. But there was no time to think about it. Jezebel was coming down the stairs . . . very slowly, very deliberately. Sarah shifted the flashlight from one sweaty hand to the other. Her legs trembled. She fumbled for the gun in the back of her pants. She had to get it out. *Now*. But it was caught on a hem or something; she didn't want to accidentally set it off. . . .

"Sarah," Jezebel whispered. She paused on the bottom step. "I figured it was you."

Sarah pointed the flashlight at Jezebel's face. *Come on!* The gun was almost free—

"Uh, would you mind?" Jezebel held up a hand and squinted into the harsh, wavering glare. She blinked a few times, scowling. Her face was very pale. Her jet black hair had never looked more wild, more disheveled. Her eyes glittered like a cat's. "I feel like I'm under arrest."

Got it. Sarah yanked the pistol free and swung it around in front of her. But it was so *heavy*— much heavier than she remembered. Her fingers were so moist, almost slimy. She couldn't hold the damn thing still. How could she possibly aim and shoot?

Jezebel chuckled. "Well, what do you know? Somebody *else* was smart enough to steal from Trevor, too." She raised her other hand. Clutched in her ringed fingers was a small, silver pistol. Sarah recognized it instantly. It was the same one that had killed Trevor.

A cold sweat broke out on Sarah's forehead. She lowered the flashlight.

"It figures." Jezebel clucked her tongue disappointedly. "Great minds think alike. It's a regular, old-fashioned, Western-style showdown. Yee-haw. But it hardly seems appropriate for the Battle of the Millennium, does it?"

Sarah's trembling finger caressed the trigger. "You're admitting you're the Demon," she whispered. "That's what you're doing."

Jezebel shrugged. "I'm not admitting anything. *You* made me whatever I am, Sarah. You and all the rest of them. I'm just the girl in the mirror. Whatever you do to me, I reflect back at you. You smile, I smile. You make a move, I make one back."

My God. She's crazy. She's totally insane—

"No, Sarah," Jezebel stated dully. "I'm not crazy. Just bored. And if you want your scroll back, I'm sorry. I don't have it anymore."

Sarah lifted the flashlight again. "Where is it?"

"Stop pointing that thing at me," Jezebel barked.

The room exploded in a white flash. A deafening, unseen force instantly knocked the flashlight from Sarah's grip. *What the—* She shook her stinging fingers. The gun nearly fell to the floor. Blackness shrouded the room. Several terrifying seconds passed before she realized what Jezebel had done: She had *shot* the light right out of her hand—

"Much better, isn't it?" Jezebel asked.

Sarah's heart slammed against her ribs. She could hardly breathe. She waved the pistol in the direction of Jezebel's voice, but she couldn't see a thing. . . .

"Now let's talk." Jezebel's tone lightened. *"You* want the scroll. I guess I can understand why. You're the Chosen One. Now let me tell you why I dropped it into the Snohomish River. You and—"

"You *what?"* Sarah interrupted, aghast.

Jezebel groaned. "You heard me. Anyway, you and all your friends were using it to frame me. You have no idea who I really am or what I really want. You twisted those prophecies to suit your own needs. Just the way Ariel twisted everything in our lives for her own selfish reasons—to make *her* look good."

I've got to make sure she keeps talking, Sarah thought frantically. She blinked and opened her eyes wide—fighting to discern *anything* in the blackness, but she might as well have been blindfolded. *It's the only way I'll pinpoint her exact location. I've just got to aim the gun straight at her voice.*

"Oh, come on," Jezebel teased. "You won't shoot me. You're not strong enough. You don't have what it takes to cut somebody down in cold blood."

Sarah shook her head. She wouldn't listen. Her teeth were tightly clenched. She gripped the gun with both hands now, steadying it . . . *controlling* it. She would prove Jezebel wrong.

"You knew this would happen," Sarah murmured. "Didn't you? That's why you made the sky black. You knew we'd have a battle, just like it said in the prophecies—"

"I *didn't* make the sky black, Sarah," Jezebel stated. "But I can't say that I'm upset about it. Or particularly surprised. Don't you see yet, Sarah? We screwed everything up. You, me, all of us—everybody on this miserable little planet of ours. This is just Mother Earth's way of saying, 'I've had enough. I'm gonna give you creeps a taste of your own medicine for all the crap you've done to me over the past three thousand years.' I'm just smart enough to use it for what it is. Me and a few others, of course. So why don't we just put our differences aside and figure this whole thing out together?"

Shut up! Sarah silently raged.

"Whatever." Jezebel giggled. "If it makes you feel better, shoot me. That's the easy way out. It's not gonna *solve* anything."

Sarah held her breath. Her finger quivered. It would be so easy—

Boom!

The gun kicked in Sarah's hands, knocking her backward.

No, no. She gasped and shook her head, stumbling. It had just gone off. She hadn't meant it. . . .

There was a heavy thud.

"You bitch," Jezebel croaked. Her voice gurgled from the floor. "You're gonna—"

A silent flash lit up the room. Sarah caught the briefest glimpse of Jezebel's face: ghastly and twisted, as if she were caught in a strobe light. Blood gushed from her mouth. But something punched Sarah in the stomach at that same moment—once, twice, three times, knocking her against the wall.

Strangely enough, she didn't hear a sound. It didn't hurt for long, either. A warm numbness spread through her body . . . and then to her head. She couldn't catch her breath. Her muscles relaxed. She slid to the floor and lay down.

Her fingers groped for the pendant around her neck, but she couldn't find it. Her hand slipped to the floor.

There was nothing she could do.

Her consciousness faded.

I did it. She mustered a final smile. *I did everything. I fulfilled the prophecy. And the scroll was right. Neither of us won. But it doesn't matter. Because the survivors did. They have the cure. The countdown is over. Jezebel is dead. . . .*

The scroll suddenly appeared before her dying eyes . . . as clearly as if she were staring at it in broad daylight: a dazzling vision of beautifully inscribed Hebrew letters, stretching off into an infinite distance—encompassing all her life had ever been.

And then, like her life, it was gone.

COUNTDOWN
to the
MILLENNIUM
Sweepstakes

$2,000 for the year 2000

5...4...3...2...1 MILLENNIUM MADNESS.
The clock is ticking ... enter now to
win the prize of the millennium!

1 GRAND PRIZE:
$2,000 for the year 2000!

2 SECOND PRIZES: $500

3 THIRD PRIZES: balloons, noisemakers,
and other party items (retail value $50)

Official Rules
COUNTDOWN
Consumer Sweepstakes

1. No purchase necessary. Enter by mailing the completed Official Entry Form or print out the official entry form from www.SimonSays.com/countdown or write your name, telephone number, address, and the name of the sweepstakes on a 3" x 5" card and mail it to: Simon & Schuster Children's Publishing Division, Marketing Department, Countdown Sweepstakes, 1230 Avenue of the Americas, New York, New York 10020. One entry per person. Sweepstakes begins November 9, 1998. Entries must be received by December 31, 1999. Not responsible for postage due, late, lost, stolen, damaged, incomplete, not delivered, mutilated, illegible, or misdirected entries, or for typographical errors in the entry form or rules. Entries are void if they are in whole or in part illegible, incomplete, or damaged. Enter as often as you wish, but each entry must be mailed separately.

2. All entries become the property of Simon & Schuster and will not be returned.

3. Winners will be selected at random from all eligible entries received in a drawing to be held on or about January 15, 2000. Winner will be notified by mail. Odds of winning depend on the number of eligible entries received.

4. One Grand Prize: $2,000 U.S. Two Second Prizes: $500 U.S. Three Third Prizes: balloons, noise makers, and other party items (approximate retail value $50 U.S.).

5. Sweepstakes is open to legal residents of U.S. and Canada (excluding Quebec). Winner must be 20 years old or younger as of December 31, 1999. Employees and immediate family

members of employees of Simon & Schuster, its parent, subsidiaries, divisions, and related companies and their respective agencies and agents are ineligible. Prizes will be awarded to the winner's parent or legal guardian if under 18.

6. One prize per person or household. Prizes are not transferable and may not be substituted except by sponsors, in event of prize unavailability, in which case a prize of equal or greater value will be awarded. All prizes will be awarded.

7. All expenses on receipt and use of prize, including federal, state, and local taxes, are the sole responsibility of the winners. Winners may be required to execute and return an Affidavit of Eligibility and Release and all other legal documents that the sweepstakes sponsor may require within 15 days of attempted notification or an alternate winner will be selected.

8. By accepting a prize, a winner grants to Simon & Schuster the right to use his/her name and likeness for any advertising, promotional, trade, or any other purpose without further compensation or permission, except where prohibited by law.

9. If the winner is a Canadian resident, then he/she will be required to answer a time-limited arithmetical skill-testing question administered by mail.

10. Simon & Schuster shall have no liability for any injury, loss, or damage of any kind, arising out of participation in this sweepstakes or the acceptance or use of a prize.

11. The winner's first name and home state or province will be posted on www.SimonSaysKids.com or the names of the winners may be obtained by sending a separate, stamped, self-addressed envelope to: Winner's List "Countdown Sweepstakes", Simon & Schuster Children's Marketing Department, 1230 Avenue of the Americas, New York, NY 10020.

Printed in the United States
By Bookmasters